Christmas Cupid

BARBARA WINKES

For D.

Chapter One

NATASHA

It was around this time of year that Natasha started dreaming about palm trees, sandy beaches and a soft ocean breeze. A colorful cocktail was part of that dream, and she had made it reality many times: Aruba, Saint Martin, and Puerto Rico. She'd browse her trusty websites and go with whatever last-minute trip offered her the most luxurious getaway for her budget.

Most of her colleagues had already decorated their houses and desks, and office parties had been booked months ago. They were running around trying to find the perfect gifts, outdo each other's decorations and dinner tables in competitions held on social media. Some might actually find happiness in that most stressful time of all, but this was the one subject Natasha wasn't curious about. Live and let live.

The resorts she booked often came with decorations and the occasional events for tourists, but unlike at home, there was little to no pressure to participate.

Her friends and colleagues might think of her habit as odd. They knew about it, and they accepted it.

Until today.

During the meeting, Natasha leaned back into her chair, wondering where Christmas would take her this year. Cancun might be an option. She had seen great offers earlier this morning.

Two more weeks, and paradise would be hers.

"Nat? Are you listening?"

She sat up straighter, aware that all eyes were on her. Okay, perhaps she needed to postpone daydreaming for a bit longer.

"Of course," she told her boss who was gracious enough not to roll her eyes. Or maybe such childish behavior was above Anna.

"Good. We all know it's been a tough year, and we need to make a big splash before it's over."

If she was talking about decadent New Year's Eve parties in the city, Natasha might be able to reach out to contacts. That could be interesting...Her smart vacation budgeting had brought her to fascinating places and helped her meet people who had been instrumental in her career. Anna always exaggerated when it came to the numbers. Everyone at the magazine had been paid their salaries as far as she knew, and there had been raises. Natasha got a raise a few months ago. Things were fine.

"Sure. What do you have in mind?"

"You ever heard about the Christmas Cupid?"

Natasha winced, a bit too obvious, as Anna's smile told her.

"It's a lovely legend that will work well around this time of year. Apparently, this woman's bakery is a place where many couples have met and fallen in love."

Natasha wasn't the only one to groan at the concept. Christmas was bad enough, Valentine's Day even worse. But the two of them combined?

"Normally I would send Ralph for this kind of story, but he won't be back before the New Year."

This made sense so far. Ralph was the guy for romance. He and his wife had a new baby, and he was taking time off for the holidays.

"What about Jen?" Natasha asked, well aware that she wasn't making these decisions. Anna didn't have many other options, as everyone knew Natasha was never available for the cutesy, tearing-at-the-heartstrings type of narrative people wanted to read during the season. It wasn't that she wanted to be contrary. She was good at her job, just not—this.

"Jen already has a long-term assignment. No, this has to be quick, so we'll have it for the website. We need to increase traffic and online subscriptions. Someone has to go to Pinedale and take a look at that bakery, meet Ivy and—"

This time Natasha was the only one to sigh. Ivy. Of course.

"I want you to do it."

"What?"

Natasha realized a heartbeat later that she was on her feet. No, she wasn't overreacting. Anna's suggestion had triggered a flight or fight reaction that everyone knew was quite normal for her. She couldn't run, so she might as well stay and argue.

"No."

"What do you mean, no?" Anna wasn't amused or even receptive to Natasha's protest. "I wasn't asking."

Colleagues around the table were focusing hard on their notes or whatever they had in front of them. Natasha couldn't believe it. She'd been working for Anna over five years, and this had never been a question. She delivered deep, meaningful stories all year round.

This wasn't for her, this wasn't *her*. Anna had to understand that she was the worst possible person for the job.

"I can't do it. I mean...I literally can't do it. I wouldn't be good at it."

"Then try. Work harder. Here, we invest in you, all of you. We've also had a lot of challenges in the past year, and if we can't improve our profile, and the numbers, we might have to reduce staff. I'm sorry, but that's the way it is."

Those images, the chair by the beach, the sunset, the ocean laid out in front of her...They burst one by one.

"Is it really that bad?"

"You think I'm making this up?"

"No. Sorry," Natasha mumbled. Come to think of it, Anna wasn't prone to empty threats. "I guess I have no choice then. I'll give it a try." Resigning to the inevitable, Natasha sat back down.

"Thank you, Nat. I knew I could count on you. The details will be on your desk. You'll be leaving for Pinedale the day after tomorrow."

"Okay. Thanks."

"And try to look a little less like we're sending you to prison?" Anna advised. "You'll be getting free cookies and hot chocolate by the fireplace. I would trade places with you if I could."

Some murmurs from the group indicated that they sided with Anna. Traitors.

"All right." She didn't mean it, but the alternatives didn't look any better.

"You'll be fine," Anna said, sounding relieved. "Now, let's move on."

Natasha didn't pay much attention to the rest of the meeting. She didn't daydream about her plans for the season either, because they had just gone downhill. This was the first time Anna had gone against her instincts and all reason.

What Natasha disliked most about Christmas was that so many people engaged in fake cheer, harboring high expectations that could never be fulfilled. It always ended in tears.

Now she had to pretend to be interested in all of it and do a good job. Be fake.

Before she returned to her desk, Natasha made a beeline for the break room—someone had put up a small tree here too, of course—where she got herself a coffee and a chocolate bar. Then she went to face the inevitable: The incredible Christmas Cupid, a woman named Ivy who had found a grand marketing strategy for her baking business.

IVY

Seeing all the tables in the small café filled, many of them with couples, always put a smile on Ivy's face. A wealth of love, and otherwise. She earned more with the bakery than with the job she held for the rest of the year.

She would never forget the first time she came back to Pinedale to open the *Magic Christmas Bakery*, October to February, the way her mother and grandmother had done it before her. Friends and family had warned her she was taking a big risk for a fairy-tale, but six years later, she had convinced them all.

The magic was still alive, and always would be.

Taking that risk had paid off for her.

She cast a glance outside the window where snow was softly falling. The darkened sky made it look and feel later than it was. Ivy loved the town in lights on an afternoon like this, when everyone was still busy, but the images told of a slower, more reflective time to come. Time to breathe. To heal.

In the midst of all this, she could put a smile on so many faces with her grandmother's recipes that were unfamiliar to a lot of her customers. They came for the cookies, cakes, hot chocolates, and maybe a little extra. Maybe they would find the one.

Ivy breathed in the scent of spices and cocoa. She wished she could live and work here all year long, that the sweet anticipation of Christmas wouldn't come only once a year.

As it was, she had to seize the moment. Ivy had been working on putting together a book with Oma's Christmas delicacies, and she was going to meet a reporter from out of town the next day.

Until then, she had a lot of baking to do.

Before she went back to her workstation, Ivy noticed a little girl standing in front of the display behind the counter, admiring the selection: Heart- and tree-shaped cookies, chocolate covered candies and sweets, various types and forms of gingerbread. The children always brought her back to her grandmother's kitchen, where her fascination with measurements and the chemistry of baking had been born. Magic. That's what it was all about. Just like when two people found one another and knew.

Ivy wasn't sure if the latter could happen to everyone, but she knew without a doubt that the handwritten recipes always worked without fault. She would stick to the chemistry in the kitchen. Given how many people came for the sweet treats she created, that would keep her busy for another year.

Ivy picked up a pair of tongs and a paper bag and put one of the heart-shaped gingerbread cookies inside. She handed it to the girl whose whole face lit up as she beamed.

"You have to try these," she said with a wink. "Merry Christmas."

The mother thanked her and went on to buy a dozen.

Mrs. Whitmore's knitting cycle was here as well. Ivy knew they always bought an abundance of baked goods to take home.

It was a good day. Christmas was around the corner, and the advent time was beautiful the way it always was in Pinedale.

Why was she nervous?

Back in the kitchen, Ivy took some dough out of the fridge and started rolling it, knowing that the staff she had hired the second year was more than capable of minding the store.

With the familiar task, a sense of calm returned. It was the most wonderful time of the year. This time would be no different.

Chapter Two

NATASHA

S uppressing a curse when the alarm woke her at a quarter to six, Natasha stumbled out of bed and headed for the shower. She could have slept a bit longer if she had packed the night before, but she didn't feel like it. After a dinner with friends who hadn't been as supportive of her complaints as she'd hoped, she came home and went straight to bed.

While the coffee was brewing, she tried to put together what she hoped were acceptable outfits for the town of Pinedale, the disappointment still crushing. Usually, her luggage included sundresses, shorts and sleeveless shirts, and bikinis. From her preliminary research Natasha knew that she had to prepare for even lower temperatures than what she was used to in the city. She'd be freezing on top of it all, great.

She would be taking the first train out of town—Pinedale had a train station, but no airport, so the trip was only slightly longer, without the waiting time.

When Natasha arrived at the train station, dawn was just breaking, few other passengers on the platform. She had bought another coffee and a pastry for breakfast to accompany the reading she still had to do.

By the time the train arrived, she was already shivering. It could only get worse from here...At least there was no one sitting next to her, and she had space to work.

With her laptop in front of her, and notes spread out, Natasha had little time to enjoy the view of decorations and the coming sunrise. She was miserable and would be for a while to come, the buttery pastry only a small consolation.

Anna had mentioned baked goods. They had better deliver, because what more could Ivy offer her that she couldn't find here in the city?

The *Magic Christmas Bakery* had a website decked out in the traditional colors, with a picture of the owner smiling into the camera. She was cute, Natasha had to give her that—and a smart businesswoman if she could make the cupid narrative work for her and boost her sales of cookies and cakes.

Not cute enough for Natasha to be any happier with her assignment. She would get it over with as soon as possible and deliver the best story she could. If she was lucky, there would still be time for a week under the sun, all-inclusive, somewhere.

The time flew by as she read up on Ivy, who had been gifted a box of handwritten recipes from her grandmother and decided to share them with the world. Sure, they were special to her, but it took Natasha only a few minutes to find a myriad of blogs and recipe sites with pictures that looked fairly similar. They didn't claim any magic touch or particular matchmaking talents.

Natasha leaned back in her seat, pensive. Anna wanted a romantic human-interest story, but what if the story was something else altogether? She wasn't ready to assume it was all a hoax—not yet—but she didn't believe that people were more prone to falling in love in that place either. People believed what they wanted to believe, and they might be more receptive when high on the comfort and joy sugar provided. Add a few lights and a little music...

There might be a way she could put a generous spin on it, so Anna wouldn't fire her outright: *Local Businesswoman Finds A Charming Way To Promote Bakery*. She cast another glance at Ivy's picture.

Charm or con? Natasha was about to find out.

·♥·♥·♥·♥·♥·

She changed trains for the last time after two and a half hours, only to have ninety more minutes to go. Nestled into a hillside and surrounded by woods, Pinedale was the last stop on the route. Around noon, Natasha packed away her work and leaned back to close her eyes for a bit.

"Ma'am?"

Jolting awake, she thought the train had filled up all of a sudden and she'd have to make room, but instead she realized the conductor was standing in front of her.

"This is the last stop."

"Oh. Okay. Thank you." Scrambling to get her coat and luggage, Natasha got off the train, finding a corner where she could zip her coat and arrange her scarf against the biting wind.

Gray clouds were low in the sky, signaling that the flurries were only a fraction of the snow that was going to fall in the next few hours. Glancing at her watch, Natasha hoped she would get a cab right away, or she wouldn't be able to check into her Bed & Breakfast before meeting Ivy.

Seeing a driver waiting in his car when she left the station, Natasha hurried her steps, but a family of four snatched the only cab from her. She resisted the urge to stomp her foot. Everything had gone wrong after Anna's announcement. It made her wish she'd missed the meeting.

"That happens sometimes."

She spun around to see the train's conductor whose shift had apparently ended.

"And what do you do when that happens? I have an appointment in Pinedale in a little over an hour."

He looked pensive. "That might be cutting it close, but I could take you up."

She narrowed her eyes. "Why would you do that?"

He seemed as puzzled by her question as she was by his suggestion.

"Why not? It's no trouble. I'm Jake. You must the reporter coming to talk to Ivy?"

Talk about puzzled. "How do you know?"

"It's a small town. Come on, let's get you to your hotel. You don't want to miss out. Ivy's place is fantastic."

"So I've heard. Thank you."

"Like I said, it's no problem."

Jake had been right in one thing—they were cutting it close. When they arrived at the B&B, Natasha had less than half an hour to check in, get ready and find the *Magic Christmas Bakery*. The latter shouldn't be hard. Jake had driven along a street close to the small center of the village and pointed out that it was only a block away.

To Natasha's relief, he hadn't tried to make small talk or much conversation otherwise.

"Thank you," she said. "I really appreciate it."

She would book a cab for her return right away at the B&B. Natasha couldn't have this happen again. She needed to be done with the story and be out of town by Christmas.

New Year's in the Caribbean? That, too, had a nice ring to it.

She would have loved to take a hot shower and sleep some more, her wish only fueled by the even heavier snowfall. It was only after four p.m., but the weather conditions and omnipresent Christmas lights made it feel like night.

At least this wouldn't take too long. Per email she had confirmed that she'd meet with the bakery owner and discuss the following days. Natasha was hopeful that afterwards she could find a place somewhere to get a burger or pizza, and then sleep until noon the next day. She'd find time to organize her notes and start writing in the evenings, send a first draft to Anna, and get out of here as soon as she could.

A few couples had hooked up over hot chocolate and cookies. How long could that story be?

Chapter Three

NATASHA

Natasha bundled up against the cold once more and headed out, directions she had looked up on her phone, in mind. From the street of the B&B she walked down two blocks to Main Street where the *Magic Christmas Bakery* was located near the marketplace. As she'd expected, there was the town hall and a church, a few other businesses and living space above them.

The lights on the huge Christmas tree in the center were slightly dimmed under the snow, branches bending under the weight. It looked perfect for the surroundings, Natasha had to admit. It just wasn't her thing.

Three buildings down from the town hall, she found her destination and opened the door. At first glance, it looked like every other bakery during Christmas time. Natasha watched the occupants of the adjacent café, a few families and single persons, but mostly couples. Of course.

"You're here! Perfect. Natasha, right?" She turned to the other woman who was chatting away. "I'm Ivy, but you know that already." Natasha had imagined her taller. Ivy reached out a hand. "So, you've come all the way to hear more about the Magic Bakery?"

I was forced to do so, but yes.

In the face of this much enthusiasm Natasha held back any sarcastic retort that might be on her mind.

"I hear that something magical is allegedly going on here. I'd be happy to learn more."

"Sure. How about we go somewhere quieter? I have something prepared for you."

"That wasn't necessary. All we have to do today is come up with a possible schedule."

Ivy laughed. "I don't know about yours, but that might take a while already. Let's start you off with a snack."

Natasha wanted to protest, but her loudly rumbling stomach belied her intentions.

"Okay. I'm curious."

"Follow me. To be honest, I was looking forward to a little break myself. You'd think that surrounded by all these treats I get to eat a lot of them, but the truth is often I don't even have the time."

Natasha felt a bit dizzy. Perhaps it was because of all those delicious smells on an empty stomach, or the fact that Ivy was talking a lot. She led Natasha to a room in the back, an office with a sitting area that was decorated as the rest of the bakery.

"Please, have a seat."

Natasha nearly sighed in bliss when she got to sit down in one of the red armchairs.

"Just one moment, and then you'll have my full attention." True to her word, Ivy returned only a couple of minutes later with a tray that held tiny cups with what looked to be samples of hot chocolate, and a selection of cookies.

That was it? The magic?

Natasha was grateful to be in a warm and cozy place for the moment, but the cynic in her wouldn't be silenced.

"First of all, thank you for having me," she said. "I read on your website that you're here for about four months every year. When did the bakery became famous, and why?"

Ivy still had that warm, serene smile on her face. There was nothing calculating that Natasha could detect, but maybe she was just that good.

"You must know that the idea has been around for much longer, but we'll get to that, I promise. I wanted to warn you that one of these hot chocolate samples is a bit boozy. This one has Irish Cream liquor in case you don't like that. The other ones are safe."

"That's fine. My B&B is close."

"All right. On your plate is a *Zimtstern*, a *Dominostein*, a gingerbread pretzel with dark chocolate, and a piece of *Stollen*. Traditionally there are raisins in it, but my grandma didn't like them, and neither do I. She used marzipan, nuts, and dried cranberries, and that's what I do as well."

It might be the long trip, but Natasha didn't understand a whole lot.

"What are those words you're using?"

Her dry tone did nothing to discourage Ivy. "You read that my Oma, my grandmother, came from Germany? I translate everything on the menu, but those are the words she used, so I have them on my brain all the time. The cookie is made with cinnamon and a glaze, these candies are gingerbread, apple jelly and marzipan underneath the chocolate, and the *Stollen*...it's some sort of bread, with dried fruit and nuts."

"A fruitcake, basically." She had finally understood something.

"Not exactly, but perhaps the closest." With a rueful smile, Ivy shook her head. "I'm sorry, I didn't mean to start with a vocabulary lesson. How about you try them? Oh, and I forgot about the *Baumkuchen* which translates to tree cake."

"I'm going to write a glossary for our readers." It was hard to be impatient or annoyed with the woman who seemed so much in her element, happy, someone who had turned a family tradition into a successful business.

Natasha tried a bit of everything, fascinated by the combination of spices and ingredients. Most of them were familiar, but she'd never tried any of those particular baked goods.

"These are all pretty good," she said. She might have to bring some of that tree cake home with her. "I understand that you can't get them homemade in many places, so there's an appeal. How is this connected to people falling in love in this place?"

"I'm not sure I can answer that question. It just seems to happen here all the time. Customers come in, they stay for a while, chat, try something new...and they look at a stranger, and sparks fly."

Natasha was struck by the longing in Ivy's voice, real as if she truly believed her cookies and cakes facilitated new relationships.

"How many times has this actually happened?"

"Many times. I mentioned it on my website, but in order to see it, you have to come here to Pinedale. People send me pictures and notes or bring them to me when they return. There used to be a wall here in the café with all of them, but we ran out of space. They're part of the town museum's permanent exhibition now."

"Wow." Eventually she'd have to come up with more and better words. At the moment, it was all Natasha could think.

A legend grown out of a family tradition had made it into the museum? Of course, given the size of Pinedale, that claim to fame was relative.

"It's pretty impressive. I can show you another day."

"Yes, thank you, I'd like that." From what Natasha had seen, there wasn't much to do around here. The more she filled those days, the faster they'd be over. She had to admit though that talking to Ivy and tasting her work had been the highlight of her trip so far.

She still would have preferred cocktails on the beach, but she had bills to pay.

"Great. I'm afraid I'll have to get back to the kitchen soon, but perhaps you'd like to join me around four?"

"Tomorrow afternoon?"

"Four a.m., when I get started. I promise you it will be interesting for your article."

Natasha hoped the sheer horror she felt at the notion wasn't showing on her face. After this, Anna owed her, big time.

"I suppose I can make that happen..."

"Don't worry. I know this takes a bit of time to get used to. It took me a while to adjust. Now I'm lucky to have enough staff so I don't always have to be there around the clock, but I still enjoy it. A new day, a new beginning..."

"You've been writing a book, and you still have the café. When do you sleep?"

The longer this conversation lasted, the more Natasha realized she would be hard pressed to find the angle she imagined. Yes, Ivy was successful and passionate about her business, but nothing about the Christmas bakery seemed like a calculated ruse for the gullible. Whatever was happening here, Ivy truly believed in it.

Natasha found herself intrigued and irritated in equal parts—which was a lot more intrigued than she had imagined.

21

It might have to do with Ivy, the Christmas Cupid herself. A picture and a few paragraphs on a website didn't do her and her idea justice.

"Not much while I'm in Pinedale, that's for sure. But it's wonderful in the truest sense of the word, so I don't want to miss a thing. I can now afford to do my regular job on a part-time basis, so I can relax a bit, but I always love coming here."

"You ever think about moving here full-time?" There were still pieces of the story Natasha didn't understand. Some of them were likely unrelated to the holidays, and those were the parts that had her most curious.

"Oh, all the time, but it wasn't meant to be, at least not so far. The Christmas bakery has always been open for the same length of time...that's how the magic works. It's not up to me to mess with that."

"Can I be honest? I'm not sure if you're serious."

She'd found the right tone. Ivy didn't take her statement to heart.

"I'm not always sure either. There's a huge wall in the museum with proof that people found each other here. They came in because they heard about the sweet treats, and they found love. My grandmother didn't know why, neither did my mother. We just bake and are along for the ride, somewhat, at least. It's rewarding to see people happy."

"I can imagine." Something about that struck Natasha as uncomfortable. She'd never met anyone like Ivy. Most people she knew, including herself, tried to walk through life without hurting anyone, at least not on purpose. That seemed a far cry from upending your life for four months every winter to make people happy. Never ask why.

"This might sound a bit nosy. Did anyone in your family find love because of the Christmas cupid?"

"I wouldn't say nosy, but I really have to get back to work. Actually, the answer is no. I'm sorry. We can continue this tomorrow? I'll have strong coffee and breakfast ready."

"Sounds like a plan. Thank you."

Natasha sensed the evasion behind the polite smile. Perhaps she had found her angle.

·♥·♥·♥·♥·♥·

Walking home along light-filled windows, Natasha pondered what she'd just learned. If it was all coincidence, how did the bakery get a whole wall in a museum? She didn't think Ivy's cheerful attitude was an act. For sure, she didn't need to be in a relationship to be happy and pursue her dream.

Natasha was proof of that, wasn't she? She went on dates on occasion, enjoying the company, the effort that both sides put into it, choosing the perfect place and outfit. After a lovely dinner, they usually went their separate ways, and she was okay with that.

She realized she had forgotten to ask about a place to eat. Sampling the delicious treats had been fun, but they'd been just that, samples. She didn't want to wait until the next morning and breakfast Ivy had promised for...*Heaven help me*. Four a.m. Even during her vacations in paradise, she never got up early enough to see the sun rise.

At the end of Main Street, a small restaurant advertised comforting and traditional dinners for the season. She hadn't seen any place for burgers or pizza yet, and the snow was still coming down, so, turkey dinner it was.

When she walked in, Natasha realized that it was even smaller than it had looked from the outside. She usually tried to avoid places like this, because people were far too chatty.

Within seconds, a woman in her mid-thirties, wearing a bright smile, came heading her way.

"Good evening. You picked quite the night. How many?"

Again, not my choice.

"Just me, thanks."

The woman pointed to a table close to a fireplace with an old-fashioned mantel. To the right was a window to the back-yard where Natasha saw lights on a tree and hills in the distance. She suppressed a yawn. It was all rather idyllic. Just not her kind of idyllic. She would have grilled fish, rice, and fresh mango for dinner if all had panned out, and a different view.

Not this time. Not yet.

"Will this be okay?"

"Yes, thank you."

Natasha realized that a few of the other patrons cast intrigued glances her way. She remembered Jake, the conductor, wondering how word about her arrival had spread this fast in Pinedale. Then again, there didn't seem much to this town beyond Main Street.

She sat down and, when the waitress arrived, ordered the turkey menu for simplicity. After the sweet afternoon, it seemed appropriate. Then she started jotting down notes. *Baker found her calling in charming surroundings... The Christmas Cupid. Comfort & Joy, and the occasional wedding. Ivy bakes.* Young, successful...*attractive*...

Now that didn't have any place in her article. Pinedale was not the right setting to start flirting, especially not with someone who was in love with Christmas and romance.

Worst timing ever. Wrong time, wrong place.

She looked up to see the waitress carrying a plate Natasha could only describe as giant, with all the bells and whistles: A generous piece of turkey, stuffing, cranberry sauce, mashed potatoes and gravy, and roasted Brussels sprouts on the side.

Everything looked delicious, and like it was enough for two.

"There you go. I hope you enjoy."

"Oh, I know I will. Thank you."

This might be a mistake, since she'd have to get some sleep soon and get up at an objectionable time, but Natasha was willing to risk it. Everything looked and smelled too good. She couldn't remember when she'd last had a dinner like this.

Or maybe she could, and that was the problem.

It wasn't much of a surprise given that she'd been forced to travel to Christmas Central, which was almost like traveling back in time. She never dwelled on memories when watching the sun set on the beach.

Chapter Four

IVY

Approximately eight months of the year, her life was fairly bland and uneventful. She did her job as a customer service agent and socialized with colleagues as much as she had to, polite small talk and occasional dinners. Then her other life began all over again, and she could escape to the beauty of Pinedale where snow at Christmas was guaranteed, and people from all over the country flooded the *Magic Christmas Bakery* for a piece of gingerbread, and that magic.

She tried out new recipes from the box when at home. During those months in Pinedale, she had to produce.

It was different from those relaxed afternoons in her Oma's kitchen, but she loved it nevertheless. Pinedale, with those hills around it and the early fall of dusk in the winter felt like a protective blanket, like nothing and no one could hurt her there—and that brought back that childhood memory without fail, even though it was a bit more hectic.

When she headed to the bakery that morning, the tension she'd felt yesterday hadn't entirely left her. Ivy wasn't sure if she could blame her state of mind on the new arrival, Natasha. She had occupied Ivy's thoughts since the moment she'd walked into the bakery, looking gorgeous and a bit lost in the small town.

What was she afraid of? Ivy wasn't intimidated by the fact that Natasha lived and worked in a big city—the same was true for Ivy for most of the year. She seemed a bit skeptical when it came to the Christmas Cupid legend. Ivy had been at some point in her life. She had accepted that it was real and that it did work, for the many people whose *thank you* notes, and pictures, were displayed in the museum. And for many more to come. She didn't need to question it.

If Natasha did, that was her problem. All Ivy wanted was to make her customers happy, and given the feedback she received year after year, it was pretty clear she did. There was no need to worry. They were both professionals. They'd do their jobs, and Natasha would go home. As usual, Ivy would stay until the end of February when the Italian family, who took over her bakery/shop for two thirds of the year, returned.

No big deal.

Except when the clock on the wall showed 4:10 a.m., and there was still no sight of Natasha, she couldn't help feeling disappointed. Had she already given up on the story? Had Ivy bored her?

East Coast Magazine had approached Ivy, not the other way around. If Natasha didn't want to be here, why didn't they send another writer?

Ivy wrestled with those questions a little while longer while she got a first batch of gingerbread and sugar cookies into the oven, until a knock on the door startled her.

Natasha looked apologetic.

28

"I'm so, so sorry. I don't usually screw up like this. Can I come in?"

"Of course. I have to keep an eye on these cookies, but I'll start the coffee. For breakfast, would you prefer eggs and meat, or something sweet?"

"I have to admit I went to dine at Betty's restaurant yesterday...A coffee is fine."

"Okay, maybe later then? I have honey gingerbread in the oven."

"You're tempting me," Natasha said with a smile. Maybe it was her tone, or the way she looked her up and down that got Ivy flustered. She didn't want to examine the reason.

"Well, that's my job here. It's all about temptation. How about I make the coffee, and you can just look around and ask me whatever you'd like to know? We have a bit of time before the café staff comes in."

"Sounds great." Natasha hid a yawn behind her hand. "I'm sorry. So, when did you first realize that your grandma's baked goods were matchmaking material?"

"She told me the story when I was little. Of course, for a long time, I thought it was just that, a story, but then I heard the same things from my mother. And when I started over, it kept happening. I don't know, people might be more open during the holidays...They are more focused on their hopes and dreams...What are you hoping for?"

"Me?" She laughed, as if startled by Ivy's question. "It's not a story about me."

Ivy felt her heart beat faster, and not because she'd gotten ahead of her guest. Maybe she was tired too. She had her own routine here in Pinedale, and Natasha was already interrupting it.

"But there's a reason you're here, writing about the bakery."

"It's my job."

"This particular story?"

The coffeemaker had finished brewing, and Ivy took two cups decorated with Santa's sleigh out of the cabinet. She noticed Natasha frowning at them, even though she gratefully accepted the mug after Ivy had filled it with coffee.

"You got me," Natasha admitted. "It's not my usual beat, but I don't mind something different. It keeps the writing interesting—I hope. There's your answer."

The honey gingerbread was almost ready, but Ivy didn't want to wait that long. Her nerves needed something now, so she cut a piece of the almond marzipan wreath with the apricot glaze.

"All right. You're sure you don't want any?"

Natasha cast a longing look at the plate.

"I kind of do...This trip might turn out to be more expensive than I thought. I'll have to buy a new wardrobe."

"Don't worry. If you want the full Pinedale experience, there will be a bit of hiking and ice-skating on the agenda. You'll be fine."

Instead of reassured, Natasha looked dismayed.

"You don't skate?"

After her first bite of the piece of almond wreath, Natasha closed her eyes for a few seconds.

Talk about getting flustered.

"This is amazing."

"Thank you."

"You're welcome. And no, I don't skate. To be honest, I'm not much into winter sports."

Ivy might be wrong, but the pieces were adding up. She guessed that Natasha wasn't much into winter, or Christmas. But why had they sent her then? There had to be someone at the magazine who enjoyed the holidays? She had liked the baked goods, and she had enjoyed Betty's turkey dinner as well. There might still be hope for her. Ivy felt herself smile.

"That's all right. We'll still have some walking to do if you want to learn about Pinedale, and why the bakery started here. I'll have someone take over for me at lunch, and afterwards we could go to the museum?"

"Sure. I'm curious about that wall of fame."

That was it! Ivy felt a sense of relief when she realized that it wasn't pretty Natasha that made her nervous, or her reluctance to believe in a proven theory. No, it was the change of schedule that made Ivy restless—even though she had planned ahead for it, and Tina knew exactly how to handle the bakery for a day. It had been the same when she had to admit that she couldn't run things on her own anymore.

Taking a few hours off in the middle of the season was a big deal. It had nothing to do with Natasha.

"We'll go later then. I'd like you to meet a few people too."

"Great." Natasha took a few pictures before she turned to Ivy once more. "Since we have a little more time today...You said cupid didn't strike for you or anyone in your family. Why do you think that is?"

Oh, not that again. Ivy forced a smile.

"Isn't that obvious? Whoever runs the bakery *is* the Christmas Cupid. It's not something you can do for yourself."

"Fair enough. So you're single?"

Ivy winced. "You don't need to know about that for your article."

"No," Natasha admitted. "I'm just curious and nosy. I'm sorry, you're right. That was out of line."

"I'll forgive you since you're clearly not used to being awake at this time of day. But now I have to get some work done. Do you want to learn how to make *Baumkuchen*?"

"Yes, please. And thank you for putting up with me."

31

Ivy didn't know what to say to that, so she smiled and went to assemble the ingredients. It wasn't Natasha's fault, but this was turning out to be harder than she'd thought.

She couldn't wait to take her to the museum. There, it would be all about the couples who had found love, and Ivy's own bland story would vanish into the background. This wasn't about her.

Chapter Five

NATASHA

She couldn't figure Ivy out, and it irritated her. That, and the fact that when they left the bakery, every few steps they ran into someone who knew her or knew that Natasha would be writing about the bakery—or both. Christmas was coming up. This was still the time when people tried to outdo one another, menu, decorations, and gifts. It was cold.

Could Pinedale be the only place on Earth where no one was stressed out of their minds?

Perhaps it was just the lack of sleep that made her overreact. Natasha hadn't lied. She was looking forward to seeing the museum, her first real evidence for the Christmas Cupid story.

The museum was located next door to the town hall, a three-story building with decorative elements, looking like it was one of the older structures around here. They went up the stairs, and Ivy opened the huge wooden door.

"Come on in."

In the lobby, a woman in her seventies sat behind a counter. Natasha noticed the shelves with flyers and postcards to the left. What else, beside the town square, was there to see in Pinedale?

She got up and left her place to greet them, Ivy with a hug, Natasha with a firm handshake.

"I'm Marilyn. You are the lady from *East Coast Magazine*. I really enjoyed your article on the all-women construction company."

"You read that?" Natasha asked, stunned.

"Of course. I have an online subscription, and I love your column. But today, you're here about Ivy's Christmas magic, right?"

"You could say that," she affirmed, still perplexed.

"I have the afternoon off," Ivy added. "I'll show her around the museum as well."

"Please, do. The history of Pinedale and the Christmas Cupid have always been intertwined," Marilyn said. "I was here when it first started. If you have any questions, let me know."

"Thank you. I was hoping you'd say that. We'll stop by after?"

"Sure. I still have some of your *Stollen*." Marilyn winked. "I'm sure Ivy told you all about it already, but you have to taste it. A lovely type of holiday bread."

Natasha nearly groaned. That new wardrobe was becoming more likely every hour.

"We'll see, but first I'd like to show her some things. Natasha?"

"Coming."

"I saw the look of panic on your face." Ivy chuckled as they walked up the stairs. "You know, I won't judge if you want to take a break. I'm only here for a few months each year, and people like to indulge."

"I get that. Perhaps you should launch an online shop, so they could indulge all year."

"I don't know. This kind of food goes with snow and mistletoe, not so much with your summer barbecue."

Grilled meat, a crisp white wine...Natasha lost herself in the fantasy for a moment. When they reached the top of the stairs, her jaw dropped.

In describing the wall, Ivy had not exaggerated. They were standing in front of a huge space filled with pictures of happy, smiling couples, accompanied by notes. Panels with even more notes had been added to the side. When she stepped closer, Natasha could quickly tell that all of them were full of gratitude and affection, for the town, the place where they had found each other, and the woman who had made it all possible—or so they believed.

Overwhelmed by the sudden magnitude of the story, Natasha started reading, all the way up, and to the right. Ivy waited patiently in the background. Perhaps she was used to a reaction like this, from people who were skeptical about the connection between bakery and subsequent weddings.

She stopped in front of the picture of an older couple whose first encounter at the *Magic Christmas Bakery* dated back more than fifty years.

"That was one of the first," Ivy said quietly.

Many more were recent. While most appeared to be straight couples, Natasha spotted a few same-sex couples in the crowd. Alina and Jessie. Mark and Kevin.

Thank you so much for everything!
It's been truly magic.
See you next year.
We'll be back for Christmas in Pinedale.
Our tenth anniversary!

"There are so many." Natasha laughed, self-conscious for reasons she couldn't explain. It might be that her statement sounded odd even to her, given this phenomenon was the reason Anna had sent her here.

"You had your doubts." Ivy wasn't asking. She didn't sound offended either, just matter of fact.

"I had my doubts as to what qualifies as many...I don't know what I was thinking," Natasha admitted, studying the picture of a young family, Mom, Dad, two girls perhaps three, four years apart in age. At some point, her own parents might have been happy like that, but nothing lasted forever. Even Ivy's engagement in Pinedale was limited to a few months a year.

Reality caught up to everyone eventually—didn't it?

But Ivy came back every year, and so did people hopeful for a miracle. They believed. Natasha shook her head. Anna had chosen the worst possible person for the job. Natasha was starting to feel bad for Ivy who could have gotten so much more out of this—while Natasha could be sipping cocktails on the beach. They weren't a good match.

She turned to find Ivy's gaze on her, calm, with a hint of curiosity.

Wrong, it was all wrong. Back in the city, she would have asked her out, spend a night getting to know her only to, what, run again? Move on the next safe encounter, no strings attached, no deeper meaning? Natasha didn't do one-night stands, but she didn't do many second dates either.

Why bother when you knew where it would lead already? There was no magic, just learning to manage your expectations. She walked back along the wall and took a few pictures.

"This should do for now. Thank you for bringing me here. It's impressive."

"I'm glad you think so...You're not easily impressed."

"That sounds a bit like a backhanded compliment, but I'll take it. There is definitely something going on in Pinedale, and I'm sure our readers will be intrigued. I still think you should have an online store. I agree those aren't summer treats, but you could take orders early and go beyond your February deadline."

"I'll think about it. Would you like to see a bit more?"

"Sure. Marilyn said something about the bakery being connected to the history of Pinedale?"

"Yes." They walked past the wall into another room filled with black and white photos and framed newspaper articles. "As you know, my grandmother came from Germany. My grandfather's ancestor founded Pinedale, and we had a few mayors in the line. My great-grandfather left Pinedale with his family to see the world. His son, my grandfather, stayed in Germany to study, and that's where he met my Oma. They came back here and started the bakery."

"Why only four months? Why stop for years in between?"

Ivy's smile faltered, but she composed herself right away. Natasha waited as she tried to come up with an answer.

"It's a lot."

That sounded like there was a much longer story. Natasha hadn't given up—or, at best, postponed—her usual vacation paradise for a non-answer like this.

"How?"

"How about we finish up here, and then we talk to Marilyn? You might want to take a nap afterwards, and I'll have to check on the bakery."

"Of course." *We're not done.* Natasha wanted to know what had caused that flash of sadness in Ivy's expression. To her surprise, she wanted to know if she, or her article, could make it any better. Why? She didn't look too hard for a reason. While she was here, taking up Ivy's time, she might as well be useful. "I was wondering though if I could take you out to dinner?"

If Ivy was surprised, she didn't let it show.

"You don't have to do that."

"I know, but I want to. I'm aware I'm upending your schedule. Let me show my appreciation."

"All right. I can bring you a few photos you might want to use in your article."

"Perfect." Natasha looked back over her shoulder at the wall of joy. Something didn't add up, and she'd find it. If that required spending more time with Ivy, she didn't mind.

Chapter Six

IVY

What did that mean? Had Natasha just asked her out on a date, after they'd known each other less than twenty-four hours? No. She almost laughed out loud at her foolishness. She was going to show her appreciation, because Ivy made time for the article.

As they sat with Marilyn for coffee and some *Stollenkonfekt*, bite-sized versions of the original, Ivy let her thoughts drift. It didn't mean anything that she'd felt antsy and restless even before Natasha arrived, and that her thoughts had been revolving around her. Ivy didn't date, not anymore, and she was happier for it. Even if she didn't have a reason, she couldn't imagine that a woman like Natasha would want to be with her. They both had careers to show for, and Ivy didn't suffer from a lack of confidence.

However, she was aware that her passion for Christmas, the bakery and the happiness it brought, didn't seem real to

Natasha. She lived in a different world where magic, fate and soulmates were just stories, fantasy.

Ivy should be relieved that she was leaving again soon. If they spent much more time together, some of that skepticism might rub off on Ivy, and she couldn't have that. If you didn't believe in love, what else was there?

Did Ivy?

"...went over to the bakery any chance I got. We were engaged when it first closed," she heard Marilyn say. "But everything tastes exactly the same. It brings back so many memories. Ivy is a gifted baker."

Ivy forced a smile, studying Natasha who listened with a serious expression. Until her husband's death, he and Marilyn had enjoyed a long happy marriage. Cupid didn't guarantee everything.

"I agree," Natasha said. "Even without the legend, it would have been worth the trip."

"Well, for many of us it's a little more than a legend. It changed our lives."

"Of course." Natasha's response was quick and smooth. "I didn't mean to suggest otherwise."

"Oh, you probably did—but you came here for a reason. I wouldn't be surprised if you were ready to invite a little magic into your life before you go home."

That was perhaps too optimistic. Ivy couldn't put her finger on it, but she sensed that Natasha struggled to stay polite at times. She might be going through a difficult time. Many people did during the holidays.

For Ivy, Pinedale was a place where she could recover the joy and dreams she'd experienced as a child. She wished she could give that to Natasha before they went their separate ways.

Talk about being too optimistic. There was a tension between them, and not getting into a fight over what was true and real, was possibly the best she could hope for.

"We'll see," Natasha said diplomatically. "If you're okay with that, I might come back for some follow up questions."

"That's no problem. I'm here every day except Wednesday, and Sunday morning. Opening hours differ a bit over the holidays, but you'll find everything on the website."

"Thank you so much. I'll be sure to check it out."

Both of them rose and shook hands again, and Ivy realized that she'd missed most of the interview. What was going on?

Her companion was equally as quiet as they walked back to the bakery.

"I didn't know that Marilyn was one of the people who found her soulmate here." To her credit, Natasha said the term soulmate with a straight face.

"She did."

"It's scary to think about...finding that one person and then losing them again."

"They had four decades together," Ivy reminded her. "They were happy. And she's working to preserve the memory of what Pinedale and the bakery have given her."

"Is that enough?"

That question, paired with a tone sounding almost irritated, startled and surprised her.

"I don't know. What is enough?"

They had arrived in front of the bakery, and Ivy changed gears. "You want to come in and work here for a while? Observe in the café?"

"I think I'll do that tomorrow," Natasha said, "but thank you. I'd still like to buy you dinner, but I'm afraid you'll have to choose the place if you don't want it to be Betty's again. I still have to find my way around here."

"Betty's is fine. How about I come by the B&B, and we go from there?"

"Sounds like a plan. Why don't you call me when you leave?"

"I will. Have a good afternoon—and nap."

"Thank you."

Ivy stepped into the bakery only to be wrapped into a firm hug the next moment.

"There you are! We were afraid we might miss you." Alina stepped back to regard her. "You look great—but of course you have the best job in the world. How many weddings so far this season?"

"Oh, I'm not sure. Most of the time I don't know until a few months later. Alina, Jessie, it's so good to see you."

"You too," Jessie said. "We didn't waste any time and are already planning the Christmas party, but we wanted to come here first, have our usual."

Jessie and Alina had first connected over a piece of honey gingerbread and a cup of mulled wine.

"Great. Why don't you find a seat, and I'll bring it to you right away?"

Seeing the two made her heart lighter, reminding her that little had changed regarding the coming days and weeks. Every year some of the couples struck by the Christmas Cupid came together to celebrate. She had become close friends with the group, and they invited her every year. Like Ivy, many of them didn't have any family close by to spend the holidays with. She wouldn't miss the event for anything. It was all about comfort and joy, without ignoring the grief they had experienced. It was about friendship—and love.

Ivy couldn't help wondering who Natasha would spend Christmas with as she hurried to fulfill Alina and Jessie's order. The annual party held at the museum, with the wall of joy in plain sight, was part of the true Pinedale experience, but it was yet unclear if that was really what Natasha was looking for.

NATASHA

When the alarm went off, Natasha bolted upright, disoriented for a few seconds. Like the day before, the sky was already darkening. She knew she'd be on time, but the vivid dreams from her nap were lingering. Warm sun, a soft breeze caressing her skin as she lay in the hammock, the woman she'd just met, snuggled into her arms.

"Oh no. No way." Natasha got to her feet and started pacing. This was as predictable as it was ridiculous. Ivy and her fabulous creations presented a source of comfort in this challenging situation. Christmas overload and a lack of sleep were getting to her. Natasha didn't need any more of an explanation as to why her subconscious had invited Ivy into her dream.

She didn't have the time or desire to explore the meaning any further. Anna was waiting for a first impression. Natasha spread out her notes and started typing, willing herself not to get distracted. Work. Dinner. Tomorrow she'd observe and perhaps talk to customers. That was all.

Some of those who have been struck by Cupid's arrow come back to the Magic Christmas Bakery *year after year*, she wrote. *Others chose to make Pinedale their home, a town that was founded by an ancestor of the first owner's husband. It's all sweet at Ivy's, delicious creations from her grandmother's recipes that seem to make people a bit more receptive to falling in love. Is it the spirit of Christmas? Certain spices? Or the owner who greets everyone with warmth?*

Natasha read over the paragraph, unsure. What happened to the clever marketing strategy angle of a local businesswoman? And what was really under the surface of it all, a blessing or a curse? She had to investigate some more, but she wanted to give Anna an idea.

She also had to get ready for her dinner with Ivy, so she sent a first draft to her boss and closed her laptop. This was part of her work, even if it involved a glass or two with a woman she'd been dreaming about.

But Ivy seemed as interested in a beach vacation as Natasha was in Pinedale, snow, and cold. They'd keep it strictly professional.

She dressed in a purple sweater and black slacks. The sidewalks had been cleared overnight, but ankle boots still weren't a good idea. How did people enjoy themselves when they had to wear heavy clothes? Natasha made a face in the mirror. Since she'd started doing her seasonal getaways, she hadn't skipped a year, and she liked it that way. Not enough time to dwell.

Except she had enjoyed her activities so far, discovering the bakery and the museum, and even the dinner she'd had by herself. She wasn't going to show any weakness though. This was not her scene.

Natasha cast another look at her mirror image, admitting that she didn't hate the sight, even though it wasn't a sundress on a balmy evening. The silver necklace she'd chosen fit with the plunging neckline, her outfit simple but festive enough for

Betty's. For sure, she wasn't going to have the turkey dinner again. A salad maybe.

Her phone lit up, and as expected Ivy texted her that she was on her way. Natasha picked up her purse and coat and went downstairs.

She'd go back to talk to Marilyn as well. The older woman, too, had been suspiciously silent about the reason why the *Magic Bakery* had closed twice for several years—but whenever it opened, it was a hit. If Natasha wanted the story to be the big splash Anna hoped it could be, she had some more explaining to do. And the sooner she did, the sooner Natasha could go home.

Chapter Seven

NATASHA

She had to admit she stared a little when she opened the door to Ivy and realized she was wearing a woollen dress under her coat, together with boots that came up almost to her knee.

Ivy had worn shorts and a sleeveless shirt in her dream. *Stop it.*

They were going to have a work dinner. There was no reason they shouldn't dress in a semi-formal way for it. Ivy held out a USB drive to her.

"The photos I promised."

"Oh yes, thank you."

"Okay, Betty's it is, unless you changed your mind?"

"No. I actually look forward to it all year. They have some of my favorite dishes."

"All right. Let's go then."

The street was becoming familiar to Natasha, the huge fir in the center of the marketplace, the town hall and church in the distance... "and here we are already. I think I'm becoming a regular."

"Not the worst thing." Ivy gave her a smile that made her face flush, as if she could tell what was on Natasha's mind. Inside the restaurant, the hostess Natasha had met the day before, recognized her.

"Good evening. I'm happy to see you back here. And Ivy, thank you for making the time. I'll be over for some cinnamon stars tomorrow. Maybe this year you'll find me something else to spice up things for a bit?"

Natasha perked up. Was the woman flirting with Ivy? It took her a second to realize she was talking about finding her match in the bakery. Of course. That was the sole reason they were all here. She wasn't only chasing an illusion, she was getting distracted while doing it.

Dreaming of Ivy. She needed to focus on more earthly issues. Writing that article to keep her job. Right now, once again, food.

"I'll do what I can," Ivy promised.

The hostess seated them at a different table this time, next to a window looking out on the street. Again, Natasha noticed with surprise that no one looked stressed or hurried. They walked by, stopped to talk to one another, smiling. In the city people would fight over the remaining sales items of the year to save on Christmas gifts. Odd. That was part of what she liked to get away from, and that wish had been fulfilled, if not in the way she'd imagined.

Ivy ordered duck breast with a side of potato dumplings and red cabbage while Natasha stuck with her decision to ask for a salad.

"Yes, we have a few to choose from. Curry chicken salad, cranberry orange with radicchio—"

"The latter sounds really good, I'll take that," Natasha interrupted her.

"As a meal?"

"Yes, thank you. And I'll have the pinot noir."

"Same for me," Ivy confirmed.

"Would you like a bottle then?"

"Yes, please," they said in perfect unison, holding each other's startled gaze for a heartbeat before they both started laughing.

"It's been a long day," Ivy told the woman as she handed the menu back. "Thank you."

"You're welcome. I'll be back with your wine shortly."

"So, you think you found something worthwhile for your article?" Ivy asked when they were alone again.

"That's what I'm here for, right?" The question struck Natasha as odd. "I want to do a few more interviews, but so far it all pans out. A legend, Christmas and people falling in love over sweet baked goods...I guess my boss was right. It's a story for the season."

"You don't seem quite on board with the idea."

She'd thought she had hidden it better. Natasha waited until the waitress arrived with the wine, filled their glasses and left again.

"I don't make those decisions, but I have to admit, Pinedale is growing on me." It was hard to resist. Everywhere she went, it was warm and cozy, and people were friendly. Pinedale was the epitome of the Christmas experience to the point it was irritating. And they meant it.

Everywhere she went was...Ivy.

"It's hard to resist, isn't it? If you could have chosen, where would you be right now?"

A couple of sips of the red wine, and Natasha didn't feel like holding back any longer.

"Don't get me wrong, all of this is nice. There's a time and a place for it. I usually spend the holidays on the beach, but my colleague who writes this kind of story is home on parental leave."

Ivy took the revelations in stride.

"I see," she simply said, taking a sip from her glass.

"I hope that doesn't disappoint you. The magic bakery, it's a cute idea, and it works for so many...I'll be sure to bring the point across."

Really? It was early to make promises like that. What if she learned anything that pushed the story into an entirely different direction?

The waitress brought their meals, and Natasha was momentarily distracted by the size of her bowl of salad, accompanied by a plate with bread and cheese.

Ivy laughed. "I thought yesterday's dinner had prepared you for this. There are no tiny plates in this restaurant."

"I see. This looks too delicious, so I'll just squeeze in a few extra sessions at the gym next year."

"I don't think it's necessary. But you can be here in the present and enjoy yourself first."

Ivy laying out an uncomfortable truth for her almost made her miss the obvious compliment. The latter filled her with warmth, though Natasha had to admit that being in the moment had always been an issue for her. The season and slower pace in this town was forcing her to address these subjects more than ever—even more than those times she'd been napping or reading on the beach to the sound of ocean waves.

"What about you? You're not already looking ahead to your other job, and packing up here? You never actually told me why it's only those four months."

"First of all, that's the deal I have with the owner of the building. The family that runs the restaurant for the rest of the year spends the winters at home in Italy. Aside from that...Christmas

Cupid doesn't work all year long. It's tied to the season. You can't force it."

Ivy made her statement with a straight face. If it had come from anyone else, Natasha might have had a hard time not rolling her eyes. Even as intrigued as she was with the baker, she couldn't hide her doubts completely.

"Is that why the bakery remained closed for years, because you can't force it?"

"In part, yes. But when my grandmother died, my mother was too overwhelmed with grief to take care of the business as well, so she sold it."

"I'm sorry," Natasha mumbled. She knew better than anyone how a sudden detour from long-held plans could change everything. Usually, not for the better.

"That's okay. I'm aware that you're looking for the whole story...or maybe holes in the story." Ivy gave her a smile that did little to take the sting out of her words. It wasn't Ivy's fault. They were being honest, and it turned out Natasha hadn't been that good at pretending.

"I know that you believe it, and all the people whose pictures are on the wall, do too."

"Why don't you?"

"I believe in what I can see, what is undisputable. You are talented. You have a successful business with an excellent product. I admire you for that. The rest...It's narrative. Perception. Opinion."

"You don't think love is real?"

"Not for me, not that it means anything. But we're getting way off topic."

"I think we have more in common than you might think."

"Really? You'd like to be in the Caribbean right now?"

"No," Ivy admitted. "At least not at this time of the year. I love Pinedale during the season. It makes me feel closer to my

53

family, our history, and everything and everyone that is important to me. Another time, sure, I'd love to go."

Don't even think about it.

Too late. Perhaps it was the warm atmosphere, or the delicious food and wine, but Natasha was brought right back to her dream from earlier this afternoon.

It was an illusion, fitting for her assignment here.

She wasn't falling in love...especially not at Christmas.

IVY

After the meal, Ivy walked Natasha back to her B&B to the sound of snow crunching under their boots. The weather had cleared up, the stars bright against the clear sky. The scent of smoke from wood-burning fireplaces in the air created a vision of comfort and home.

The evening could have been difficult and awkward. Instead, Ivy felt like a weight had been lifted off her shoulders. With all the revelations made, Natasha still hadn't tried to mock her or trick her into saying something that might make the story flashier.

The relaxed atmosphere at Betty's helped too—and there might be something else, something Ivy wasn't ready to acknowledge.

She loved creating an environment and food that brought others happiness. Sometimes, it could create a lot of pressure. Natasha wasn't the first one who had asked her about her own love life.

Reading between the lines, Ivy could tell that they understood each other. Love wasn't for everyone, and perhaps people like them had a responsibility to help spread it anyway. Natasha told stories to engage her readers. Ivy's creations told stories of family and togetherness. Not everyone could find their soul-mate.

"I'll see you tomorrow?" she asked when they had arrived at the B&B.

"I'll be there," Natasha promised. "I'm glad it won't be at 4:00 a.m. though."

"Lucky you," Ivy said, and they both laughed. "If you'd like to try them, we have gingerbread waffles on the menu as well."

"I didn't think I could envision any more food in my future, but here we go. Good night, Ivy. Thank you for keeping me company."

"My pleasure," Ivy said, grateful for the cold that made their cheeks red, so Natasha wouldn't see she was blushing.

·♥·♥·♥·♥·♥·

It wasn't Natasha's fault that she began her workday yawning and a bit cranky. Ivy hadn't found much sleep after spending the evening with her. She couldn't imagine spending Christmas anywhere but in Pinedale, with the snowy hills surrounding the village, the over-the-top decorations and cherished traditions.

Life wasn't always easy, so why not go all in on making it merry and bright when you could? Everyone lost a bit of that wonder along the way, the one you could still see in children's eyes. You didn't have to lose it altogether.

Was it close-minded that she couldn't imagine listening to *Jingle Bells* while in a bathing suit? Probably, Ivy admitted to herself while she was rolling out dough. To each their own. The places Natasha went to probably had events for tourists. She might meet friends who came back each year, the same as it was for Ivy.

Not everyone had a big and welcoming family to go to, and traditions differed.

Maybe it was time to admit that she found Natasha's story intriguing for a different reason, for all the wrong reasons. She was challenging everything Ivy knew, some of which she might have taken for granted.

Ivy loved a challenge. She was beginning to like Natasha a lot more than she imagined.

Thinking of Oma, and her mother, she promised she would stay on her mission to spread happiness. She wouldn't get distracted...not too much, anyway.

As promised, Natasha rang the bell a couple of minutes before the bakery opened at 7:00 a.m.

"Hey," she said, leaning close for an awkward half hug—awkward, because Ivy almost expected Natasha to kiss her cheek, unsure what her intention was. "I'm starting to get used to those early mornings."

"Good for you," Ivy said with a wry smile. Natasha had slept a few hours more, and it showed. She looked rested, determined, and...perfect. Ivy suppressed a sigh. No distractions. It wasn't easy. "Okay, you're ready for the gingerbread waffles?"

"Yes, absolutely. And I meant to tell you that I'm planning on bringing home a few of those *Baumkuchen*."

Her accent was adorable. "Sure. Just let me know what you'd like, and I'll have it ready for you. But you'll be here for a few more days?"

"Yes. I wanted to talk to Marilyn another time, and if you don't mind, I'll check if a few of the patrons today would like to share a bit of their story."

"Go ahead. I think Mrs. Whitmore and the knitting circle will be back. Alina and Jessie too, and I heard Mark and Kevin are in town as well. There are probably a few others, and you might discover cupid's latest target."

"I hope so. All of this sounds almost as exciting as those gingerbread waffles."

"You want them with orange or red wine whipped cream?"

"As much as I'd like to try the one with the wine, it's still a workday for me. How much is in there?"

"Not enough to make you tipsy, I promise. You trust me?"

"I do."

"Make yourself comfortable. I'll be right back."

Some of Ivy's staff arrived with more customers, and by the time she brought Natasha her waffles, a third of the café was already full, orders coming in at rapid speed.

"I'm sorry I don't have much time," she said. "But that's Kevin and Mark over there, and Mrs. Whitmore with a couple of friends. They are usually five." Ivy waved back to Mark who had noticed her and send a smile her way, while Kevin was talking to their daughter, an excited five-year-old ready for the delicacies of the *Magic Christmas Bakery*. Well, maybe not all of them.

She turned her attention back to Natasha who had tried the waffles with a taste of the red wine cream, the expression on her face pure bliss. Oh, why did she have to do that?

"Let me know if you need anything else, and enjoy."

Chapter Eight

NATASHA

L ike everything she'd tasted at the bakery, the promised breakfast was beyond delicious, and she didn't regret choosing the red wine whipped cream, a perfect contrast to the spice prevalent in the waffles.

She noticed that one of the men who were here with their daughter, and two of the ladies in the knitting circle had made the same choices. Natasha guessed that the family would probably be out of here sooner, so she'd try and talk to them first.

She walked over to them and introduced herself.

"I am doing a story on the Christmas Cupid phenomenon, and I was hoping you could tell me a bit about it."

"Sure. I'm Mark, this is Kevin...and Chloe." He cast a fond look at the young girl who was enjoying her hot chocolate pancakes. "She's occupied for now, so what would you like to know?"

"You met for the first time here in this bakery?"

"Oh yes. Kevin has family he was visiting in Pinedale. I got stuck during a snowstorm, and let me tell you, I wasn't happy."

That sounded much like her own story. A lot of coincidence.

"No, he wasn't," Kevin agreed, laughing. "He blamed his misfortune on every weather forecaster, Christmas and Santa himself, but that didn't change the facts."

"I wasn't too keen on Christmas or magic, but I was hungry, and what I saw in the window looked really good. I couldn't go anywhere either, so I went inside."

"I was here with my family for an afternoon snack. I watched this handsome guy going from super-stressed and impatient to experiencing pure bliss when he tasted the *Baumkuchen*. The tree cake?"

"Oh yes. I can imagine. I'm pretty fond of that myself," Natasha admitted.

"Our eyes met...My sister noticed that I was spell-bound, and she hounded me to go over to him. It was far out of my comfort zone, but when he was ready to leave, I slipped my phone number into the pocket of his coat. Cheesy, I know."

"I was already a few miles out of Pinedale when I found it, and I went back. I didn't even know if he'd be still there, but as you can see, I was lucky. We were."

"That's a beautiful story." Natasha found herself more touched than she would have thought. "Do you believe the setting helped make it happen? The bakery?"

"Are you kidding? The cupid is the reason why we're all here, isn't she?"

Natasha preferred not to pursue that subject in depth.

"It looks like it. Anyway, thank you so much for sharing. Is there anything you'd like to add?"

"Well, thank you for asking. We now come back for the annual Christmas party. Jessie and Alina have taken over the preparations, since you can see, Ivy is beyond busy."

"Yes, she's pretty amazing."

The two men shared a look and a smile.

"She is. So, we'll see you at the party?"

"I don't know yet," Natasha said, a bit taken aback that Ivy hadn't mentioned it to her. "But thank you again."

"No problem. Merry Christmas, Natasha."

"Merry Christmas to you too."

She suppressed a sigh and got up to join Mrs. Whitmore's knitting circle. "Hi, I'm Natasha…"

"We know who you are, dear," a woman with perfectly coiffed white hair told her. "If you'd like to hear stories about the Christmas Cupid, and Ivy's Oma Klara, you're in the right place."

"That's fabulous. I see you're having the gingerbread waffles. Are those your favorite?"

The women all laughed. Natasha noticed that they were of different ages, from mid-thirties to early eighties, she guessed.

"How much time do you have?"

"As much as you're willing to give me," she promised, notebook and pen at the ready.

At some point during their conversation, Ivy came by to ask if they'd like to order anything else. All the women in the knitting circle named items they were going to take home.

Natasha caught Ivy's smile on her. As if the two of them were sharing a secret, her heart started beating faster.

Too much coffee, she reasoned.

"I met my Eddie here when Klara first ran the bakery," Mrs. Whitmore said. "But we've all found happiness over three generations of the Christmas Cupid. Are you sure you can fit all of it in just one article?"

Natasha was starting to wonder the same thing. What was even more surprising was that she hadn't obsessed on her missed beach vacation in a while.

"Eddie had traveled to Europe and seen some of the Christmas traditions for himself, so when Klara came to Pinedale, he often stopped by to chat. They became friends. I had a terrible day after burning an oven full of pies which had never happened to me before. I remembered the bakery was new in town, and I ran all the way and nearly ran over the most handsome gentleman I had ever seen. We've been together ever since."

"It really works that way?" Natasha asked, perplexed and a bit spell-bound at the conviction in Mrs. Whitmore's tone.

"It's not always that fast," Bridget, one of the younger women, said. "My husband came to visit from the other side of the country, and while we never doubted the Cupid, it took us a while to figure out how we could both make a living in Pinedale."

That made sense to Natasha. Not even Ivy could stay twelve months, or at least she had chosen not to. With her skills, she could easily run the bakery all year, just add to her selection of products? *Look at you*, she thought, amused at herself. A few days ago, she couldn't leave fast enough, now she was pondering solutions for Ivy to stay longer.

"But you made it work?"

"Of course, we did. A chance like this only comes around once in a lifetime, and when it does, you have to grab it."

"Linda and I weren't too sure at first," Jocelyn admitted. "I mean, sure, it's idyllic around here, but it's a small town. Marie, Ivy's mom, assured us that people were a lot more open-minded than we thought, and she was right. They are really all about love, and being good neighbors, all year long."

"That sounds almost too good to be true." When Natasha saw the looks the women exchanged, she realized that the longing in her tone was obvious. So, yes, big deal, every once in a while, she, too, longed for something too good to be true, something special.

She couldn't complain. She had a job she loved, a cozy apartment, and enough money for a vacation once a year. What more could she ask for?

"But it is true. John and I would love to live in Pinedale full-time, but our life is elsewhere for most of the time," another woman revealed. "So, we come to visit, and..." She held up her work, a colorful baby romper, "I get the most knitting of the year done."

"But you, too, met here first?"

"We did. And Klara's marzipan cookies might have helped. I wish I could have them all year round. There's nothing like it."

Her statement was met with mild protest, as each of the women had their favorite creation, baked, or some of the chocolates and bonbons. Natasha held back a groan. Maybe there was a reason to keep this up for a limited time each year...

"The bakery was closed for a few years, twice. What can you tell me about it?"

This time, she could see them exchange surprised glances. Why was this such a strange question?

"I'm not sure what you're getting at," Linda admitted. "Life? Klara, and then Marie, had their own stories to tend to, even if they didn't start here in the bakery. They loved their families, their husbands, their children."

"They had other avenues and talents to follow," Rose added. "Klara was a singer. I think she even recorded a song once? And Marie was very good with numbers. She sold after Klara passed away, but then came back for a few years. She found another job when Ivy's dad got sick. It was safer that way for the family."

"He died?" Natasha asked, feeling light-headed for a moment.

"Oh no, they live in Fairview."

"I'm not sure I understand."

"When Klara died, all the recipes went to Marie. She was too heartbroken at first, but eventually, she decided to come here and uphold the family tradition. When she faced challenges of her own, Ivy was next in line. In a few years, who knows? You can't force magic. It doesn't work like that."

This wasn't the first time she'd heard this. Natasha felt a sense of impatience...She was beginning to get a handle on the idea of people meeting and falling for each other over sweet treats, around the holidays.

The way Ivy's family had handled the bakery over the years, decades, was still a mystery to her.

"How is it possible that they always managed to get back in?" she asked.

Another one of those quizzical glances passed between the women.

"Don't you know? They have this long-standing contract with Pinedale. Every mayor respects it, because, well, it's part of the history," Bridget explained. "Now we have the Italian family who runs the restaurant for the bigger part of the year. We also had a fast-food restaurant and a convenience store with a food counter."

"Wouldn't you like to have the bakery around all year long?"

Her suggestion was greeted with cheers.

"If you can convince Ivy, please do it." Linda laughed. "That wouldn't be too much of the magic, would it?"

"No," Mrs. Whitmore said, sounding content. "Just the right amount of it."

They all laughed though Natasha wasn't entirely sure if she was in on the joke.

As time went by, she filled pages after pages with notes. Every once in a while, another Pinedale resident or returning holiday vacationer would stop by and add their anecdotes.

Mrs. Whitmore and her circle reluctantly excused themselves.

"Thank you so much for talking to me."

"It's been our pleasure, dear. We're glad someone gives the Cupid the credit they deserve. What's more wonderful than love, right?"

Natasha wasn't sure what to do with that. One by one, they picked up their purchases at the counter and left. Natasha opened her laptop and began to type. To her surprise, she felt a smile relaxing her face, the clicking of keys was almost hypnotic.

The words were starting to flow more easily as she could fill in the gaps, names, stories, people who were happy and satisfied in their lives without ignoring the challenges they faced. She could work with that.

Maybe Anna's idea hadn't been that bad after all. Every once in a while, she and her boss had raised the subject of Natasha branching out. Natasha hadn't expected this to be the direction she'd go in, but she wouldn't back away from a challenge of her own.

Chapter Nine

NATASHA

The next day, she woke up early and decided to show her dedication to the story by showing up before the customers. Maybe another scrumptious breakfast was on her mind as well, or was it the woman who created all those goods with a lot of love and a little magic?

Taking in her mirror image in the small bathroom of the B&B, she shook her head at her antics. Everything was going according to plan, even though the premise had changed slightly. The story was coming together. With it, Natasha would make sure her job was safe. That was all that mattered, wasn't it?

She couldn't wait to see what delicacies Ivy had in the oven today, hurrying to get ready.

When she left, the sky was still dark, the streets empty, though the Christmas lights of many homes illuminated her way. Residents' electricity bills would be off the charts after the holidays, except that the people around here didn't seem to mind.

When she arrived at the bakery, Ivy's car was parked in the front, and she rang the doorbell.

Ivy opened the door to her, surprise showing in her expression.

"Natasha. Hi."

Should she have stuck to the plan and come for opening hours? Feeling foolish all of a sudden, Natasha explained, "I hope I'm not bothering you, but I was hoping I could observe you some more..."

"Sure, no problem. Come on in."

Natasha suppressed a relieved sigh as she followed Ivy inside. This could have been a lot more awkward.

"In fact, it's great that you're here," Ivy chatted, returning to the dough she was rolling out. "It seems that Tina's daughter didn't mention it to her until last night that she needs a costume for a Christmas play ASAP. She's going to come in a bit later. I could use a little help..."

"Um...I don't know. The only baking I do is biscuits from a tube."

Ivy laughed, and Natasha reasoned that it had to be the warmth of the oven that made her cheeks flush.

"Nothing complicated." She laid the rolling pin aside. "Cinnamon stars are next. See that star-shaped cookie-cutter? You could get started with that dough while I get the gingerbread out of the oven."

"Okay...I think I can handle that."

After washing her hands, Natasha started on her task, a happy sigh escaping her at the scent of the gingerbread.

"When these are baking, we can have a little snack, I promise."

"I won't say no to that." Natasha found that her small contribution made her ridiculously happy.

"Great job," Ivy praised after inspecting her cookie-cutting skills. "See the batch over there? They all need to be iced."

"Now that's not something you should trust me with..." Natasha hesitated. "I'm afraid I'm going to make a mess."

"I'll show you." Ivy's optimism and faith in her seemed to know no boundaries. Natasha couldn't say no when she filled the piping bag, gave it to her and guided her hand along the outline of the star shape. Her cheeks were burning. Definitely the oven. That was the only realistic explanation.

IVY

Having Natasha here was a relief. Ivy wistfully admitted to herself that it might be a little more than that. It wasn't a lie that she had no time to think about any deeper implications, with so much work to do.

Within a short time, Natasha had come a long way. Ivy could remember her shocked impression when she had learned what time Ivy started each morning. Now she had shown up before the scheduled time, and was decorating cookies like a pro? Well. Almost.

In any case, her work was far from a mess, and Ivy, too, enjoyed observing her.

"Time for a little break," she announced. "I made some coffee, and I think we can make it before the crew and the masses come in."

Natasha looked up, a smile appearing on her face.

Ivy couldn't say why, but her heart started beating faster.

"What is it? You said you'd go for a snack."

"Yes. It's just...I think you have a little something...flour. Here." She had laid the piping bag aside and reached out to brush her thumb over Ivy's cheek.

"I made it!" Tina, who came rushing in, declared. "You wouldn't believe it, we've been up all night, but Amy has a costume."

"Tina," Ivy said, stepping back. "Why didn't you get some rest?"

Tina made a dismissive gesture. "There's always so much to do here around the holidays. I can sleep after Christmas. I see you hired some extra help too," she added with a wink.

Her employee's arrival filled Ivy with a mix of relief and faint disappointment. However, Tina had a point.

"Yes, come take a look. Natasha has been great. We were just about to have breakfast. You'd like to join us?"

"That would be awesome, thank you."

Was it her imagination, or was it Natasha who looked a tad disappointed at that? Either way, she needed some sustenance if she wanted to make it through this day.

If Natasha was warming up to the unfamiliar setting her boss had thrown her into, that was even better.

Chapter Ten

IVY

In the course of the day, Ivy didn't have a moment to think about the morning, or to check on Natasha who had once again set up at a table in the café. She hadn't had a lot of time to consider her suggestion for an online store either.

As Christmas was getting closer, the amount of orders increased significantly.

In the kitchen, they were preparing and packing up many of them, in addition to serving the patrons in the café and customers that dropped by to buy a quick snack or dessert for later.

Many customers had asked her if there was a way to get those sweets at other times of the year, and she had to admit, not from her. Most of the items she made could be easily store-bought, or for her customers, imported. That, of course, came at an additional cost.

What if she could bake these all year long? Would it take away from the magic? Who was to say?

But those warm spices and flavors belonged to a certain time of year, together with snow, mistletoe and a moment where everything was possible, didn't they?

When the work started to wind down and the café was mostly empty, she poured a couple of cups of coffee and added a few cookies and chocolate candies on a small plate.

Ivy brought everything over to Natasha, who looked up at her with a grateful smile.

"This is for me, right?"

"Yes, it is. You've been working hard. Would you mind if I sat...?"

"Oh no, please do. Speaking of working hard, you must have been baking up a storm in there."

Ivy sat, unable to hold back the sigh as her aching back reminded her of the truth of Natasha's statement. "Most of those are now for customers who like to have something sweet at home for advent and over the holidays—or even party favors."

"Well, I don't blame them." Natasha picked up one of the chocolate candies. "I sent another draft to my boss. She hasn't gotten back to me yet, but I assume I'll be leaving in a few days. Early next week at the latest."

"But...You won't stay for Christmas?"

Somehow, Ivy realized, she'd begun to take that idea for granted. She'd even entertained the notion of inviting Natasha to the party.

"I have a lot of the material I need. I wanted to go back to Marilyn one more time, see what my boss says...and travel will be hectic on the actual days, so I better leave before that."

"I see."

"This has been terrific so far," Natasha said, holding her gaze. "I mean it. I'm grateful for the way you've opened your door to me, and your customers have been amazing. If those stories don't bring tourists to Pinedale, and new customers to the bakery, I don't know what will."

"I'm grateful too," Ivy admitted. "This will help me decide what I do in the future. I've been thinking about that online shop. Personally, I can't imagine having these in the summer, but who am I to judge anyone? Oma Klara always said those cookies and cakes were on the supermarket shelves before we had even started putting up Halloween decorations. To each their own, right?"

"Right. Look, I might be leaving soon, but you have my number and my email. If you have any questions, I think I could help...or at least I know people who could."

"Really?" Some of the pain and fatigue vanished as she realized she they might stay in touch after this.

"Why not? Look, I won't lie to you. My plans for the holidays were sipping cocktails and taking long walks on the beach, nap, maybe read a book. I wasn't prepared for any of this, the snow, the cold, the pure merriness...but you made it all a lot less painful."

Ivy had a hard time not to cringe at Natasha using the term painful. Her offer was intriguing, nonetheless.

"If I can help, I'll be glad," Natasha added.

"Okay. That's...great. Thank you."

"No problem. I might be your first customer for the online store...and the next time I spend my vacation in a resort, I'll make sure they have a good gym."

They both laughed.

"Seriously, you have to stop saying that. There's a time to exercise, and a time to indulge oneself. Somehow, I don't have time for either one," Ivy admitted with a sigh. "At home...my tree isn't even up yet."

"I find that hard to believe."

"Don't get me wrong, I love what I do, and whenever I open these doors, everything must be in place, and perfect. My temporary home here is last."

"Do you need some help?" Natasha asked.

Ivy could feel her jaw drop. "You'd like to help me decorate my Christmas tree?"

Natasha's smile was tinged with longing and melancholy. "To be honest? I'm not sure. I never even put up any decorations because I'm usually out of town. But it matters to you, and you've been so helpful. Sure, I could do it before I go home."

"I'd love that. Thank you so much."

Ivy almost felt bad for neglecting to tell Natasha that Oma Klara never decorated the tree until two or three days before Christmas, because her family did it that way. She'd catch her up eventually...She just wanted to bask in the idea for a moment.

The bell above the door signaled the arrival of another customer.

A woman entered, looked around and came right over to them. At a closer look, Ivy guessed her to be in her late twenties.

"You are Ivy?" she asked.

"Yes, that's me. How can I help you?"

"I heard that you can help people find love," the woman said. "That's what I need, but I'm not sure anyone will ever love me." Tears were glistening in her eyes.

For some, the *Magic Christmas Bakery* had been a last resort. This wasn't the first time.

"You don't have to worry about that any longer," Ivy told her. "Please. Sit. I'll be right back. We love all our customers, and we do the best we can to make life a little sweeter. Let's start with that, shall we?" She caught Natasha's startled gaze as she got up. She'd be fine.

Ivy hoped the same would be true for her newest guest.

⋅♥⋅♥⋅♥⋅♥⋅

When Ivy returned with a hot chocolate and a piece of tree cake, she found the newcomer engaged in a conversation with Natasha. Perhaps she should hire her to engage the customers and patrons? As much as Natasha had held on to her skepticism, she was good with people, and they opened up to her.

"Oh, this looks amazing. What do I owe you?"

"Nothing," Ivy said. "You're one of the winners of my Christmas lottery, so it's on the house."

Natasha's smile told her she knew Ivy had made this up.

"So, about what you said...?"

"My name's Lara." She shook her head, self-conscious. "My friends sent me here, and perhaps it's because they couldn't stand me being miserable any longer...but they paid for it, so I couldn't say no."

"Her fiancé cheated on her," Natasha said grimly. "Then the jerk turned all of his family, and some friends, against her."

"That's despicable," Ivy admitted.

"I'm sorry for my outburst earlier, but when I stepped in here, it just all came back to me. I know my friends, the ones that stuck with me, meant well, but this is all just a legend, right? People finding love?"

"Well, Natasha is here to write about it, and she found that many stories began here. There's just no guarantee..."

"Like everything in life." Lara sighed. "I can't bring myself to regret coming here though. I'm not sure I ever had a better hot chocolate in my life, and this cake is awesome."

"Thank you. You're all alone here?"

"Yes, that's how it's supposed to work, right? My friends booked me a room at the B&B. Truth be told, I mostly needed time away from it all, and it's so nice and relaxing here already."

"I have an idea, if that's not too forward...We have an annual Christmas Party with friends, on Christmas Eve. It always takes place at the museum, where all the letters and pictures from the couples are on display. The party itself is not about matchmaking or anything, just people who either live in Pinedale or come back every year. We're family to one another."

Lara's eyes widened, and for a moment Ivy thought she might have overstepped.

"I'd love to be there. You're bringing baked goods, right? And I swear I'll pay for them too."

"We'll see. Everyone brings a little something, but yes, there's always something from the bakery."

"You two hash it out," Natasha said. "I need to get going, talk to my boss."

"Natasha, can't you stay a few more minutes?" Ivy was taken aback by her curt tone.

"I'm sorry. I'll see you tomorrow."

Ivy had no choice but to let her go and direct her attention back to Lara, though she couldn't help wondering what had prompted Natasha's abrupt departure.

Chapter Eleven

NATASHA

N atasha's day had started out great. She wasn't sure she could say the same about the way it was about to end.

Do better, the header of Anna's email said. In the body of it, she wasn't holding back either, when taking apart Natasha's first draft.

That's not like you, she wrote. *It is vague and bloodless, and we still don't know if it's magic or one of the greatest cons in history. It's like you don't want to pick a side. I sent you there for a reason, Natasha. I know you can do better.*

Thanks a lot. Natasha closed her laptop and sat on the edge of her bed, wondering when naps, or longing for them, had become part of her daily routine. She had to work, get a better handle on what she wanted readers to know about the *Magic Christmas Bakery*. And she knew Anna was right, unfortunately.

Her first idea, the clever businesswoman who had found a stellar marketing strategy, seemed too cynical now that she'd gotten to know Ivy better. Even if it could read like a compliment when done right.

If she went all in with the stories she'd learned today, including Lara's...Natasha sighed to no one. Everyone, Ivy, the women in her family, and those struck by Cupid believed in a legend coming alive at Christmas.

Could Natasha share it with the world, or at least the readership of *East Coast Magazine*, and keep the beauty and romance of it intact—and when had she started worrying about it? In her experience, people could be mean about something they didn't fully understand.

The bakery and Pinedale would get a whole lot more attention if she got this right, mostly good, but perhaps...some mockery? Or was this more about her own doubts, her own eagerness to ridicule people she'd perceived to be gullible? But there were so many of them. There had to be a way to translate Christmas Cupid into a heart-warming holiday tale without making it silly and cliché. She could do it. Right? Perhaps.

It was no bigger challenge than the one Lara was facing as she tried to pick up the pieces.

Natasha frowned when she remembered why she had left all of a sudden. As intriguing as she found Ivy, the woman, she had a hard time figuring her out. She seemed to be fine with decorating her tree with Natasha, having her patrons spill all the secrets, but she hadn't invited her to the party?

And she made that offer to a complete stranger who had just walked in?

Wait a minute.

That's how all of those stories had begun, an encounter with a stranger over sweet treats...Natasha held back a swear word, well aware that she had no right to use it in this context.

Legend had it that Cupid couldn't find love in the magic bakery, but what if that was nothing but superstition? Lara had been engaged to a man, but she could be bi? Had Natasha witnessed the beginning of something the two protagonists weren't even aware of?

Come on, you know that's too far-fetched. But...what if?

Had Natasha missed her chance?

Why would she even think that?

It was time she went home. Tomorrow, she'd meet with Marilyn. She had to buy a train ticket. Or she could book a flight and arrange for a cab ride to the nearest airport. She wouldn't have any scenic views, but she'd get home faster.

Maybe even check for last minute offers to head south. Once Anna had approved her story, she could still revisit her earlier plans.

For sure, Natasha would help Ivy if she ever asked. By that time, there would be safe, geographical distance between them, and the memory of Pinedale would be a faraway dream.

She felt a pleasant shiver skittering down her spine as she recalled *that* dream, Ivy in her arms, the sound of waves lulling them to sleep.

No. None of this was real—and she had to find someplace for dinner. When in doubt, go for more food.

·♥·♥·♥·♥·♥·

Natasha passed by Betty's and walked along the street to the marketplace with the town hall and the Christmas tree in lights. For the first time, she noticed the small pub nestled between buildings, a wreath with red bows and glass ornaments on the door. The sign was small enough it could be easily overlooked. She heard voices inside, so Natasha opened the door and stepped over the threshold.

The inside was rustic, lots of wood, a narrow staircase leading to an upper level. Whoever chose their seat there had better not get a lot to drink, she surmised.

"Natasha, hi!"

From a table in the back, she saw Bridget wave. She and Rose sat with two men Natasha assumed to be their respective husbands, and two women Natasha hadn't met yet. Chances were they were all connected to the bakery, and invited to the party, she thought glumly. This was what she'd been trying to avoid, but Bridget indicated for her to come over. Reluctantly, she went.

"Good evening. We just got here. Would you like to sit with us?"

"I'm not sure I—"

"Oh, please do," one of the unfamiliar women said. "I've been told you're a lot of fun to hang out with, and you might want to help us prepare a surprise for Ivy? I'm Jessie, by the way, this is Alina."

Everyone around the table gave encouraging nods, and once more, Natasha had no choice.

"I had a lot of fun too. So, what can you recommend here?"

"Everything," Jessie claimed. "But since the holidays are coming, I'm going with a sandwich tonight. They have some great flatbreads too."

Natasha thought of all the holiday food she'd already consumed.

"Sounds great." No alcohol tonight either. Something told her that she might have a lot more in her future, probably alone in her apartment—or if she was lucky, on a Caribbean beach. Somehow, the "alone" part bothered her more than it ever had before. Even here, surrounded by lovely strangers.

·▾·♥·♥·▾·♥·

At some point that evening, Natasha had given up on her no alcohol rule. This was why her first order the next morning at the bakery was a mug of hot, black coffee. Ivy was nowhere to be seen, but her friendly employee brought the coffee within a couple of minutes.

Natasha put her laptop on the table but left it closed, and started near inhaling the hot beverage instead. She hadn't answered Anna yet, but instead continued to write. She needed to get back to her with a new, improved proposal soon, so she could book her trip home. A couple more days at best. She had agreed to contribute to Ivy's gift, and she was going to help her decorate, but that would be it for her.

Natasha knew that her next draft would be better, and she could always finish it from home. If fact, Anna would probably appreciate that.

When she considered herself awake enough, she powered up her laptop and opened her file.

This time, the tone was different, bright, but with a hint of melancholy. Even if the story worked out, there was no lifelong guarantee for anyone. Marilyn was a widow. Rose and John would have liked to live in Pinedale but couldn't yet make it happen. Linda's parents hadn't spoken to her since she'd told them she'd be marrying a woman.

Love happened. There was no extra security.

Her mother had loved her father no matter what had happened afterwards.

If Ivy asked her to stay over Christmas, Natasha might have. Instead, Ivy had made the offer to another woman who'd all but stumbled into the bakery the day before.

Who was she to stand in the way of Christmas Cupid?

She would go home with the knowledge she already had coming here: It wasn't for her.

IVY

P art of Ivy's workday went into preparation for the party. This event mattered to her even more than serving customers and patrons and facilitating the occasional love story. She wouldn't have to provide all of the food and drinks, but it seemed that every year more people squeezed into museum to share the experience—and all of them knew about the *Magic Christmas Bakery* and its famous treats.

Some stayed only for a short while, to be a part of it all. Others were there the whole time. Everyone contributed a little something, whether resident or visitor in Pinedale.

Each year, Ivy would host a couple of dinners the same week, because the leftovers would be far too much. By New Year's Eve, most of the guests would be gone or celebrating in their own homes, and when she closed the bakery on that day, Ivy would take a day and a half for herself, to reflect, to make plans for the next year.

For the bakery and the business in general, of course. Ivy didn't make any other plans.

She had brought a sandwich from home, anticipating that she wouldn't have time to go out or sit with Natasha. She remembered that the latter had scheduled another interview with Marilyn, so she might not even come by. The thought filled her with disappointment that was gone the moment she saw Natasha sitting at what had become her usual table.

Ivy wasn't fooling herself any longer. She loved seeing her every day, and not just because Natasha could help her career in many ways. Ivy loved to spend time with her, to listen to her...She suppressed a sigh. This was where it would end. Natasha had come far out of her comfort zone. She would go back to a home, job, and favorite way of spending her vacation that was very different from Ivy's.

There was no way Ivy could let a whole year lapse, though she was curious what it would be like to spend Christmas on the beach. It was unlikely she'd find out within the next few years.

One of the bakers she had hired to help in the kitchen, called for her, and Ivy went back in. The next time she had a moment, Natasha was gone.

Was she really serious about helping to set up the Christmas tree? It had to be soon if Natasha wanted to go home early next week. And why was she hesitating? Did she really think Natasha was mad at her for some reason?

Lara was back, sitting at a table by the window. Ivy did a double-take and then smiled when she saw that she was not alone.

Ivy hadn't seen the man with her before, but he looked at Lara as if she was the only person in the world.

Ivy could feel her eyes well up, which might have nothing to do with the fact that Christmas Cupid had struck again. She guessed there would be one more person at the party—if not the one she would have loved to see there.

Chapter Twelve

NATASHA

Marilyn was busy with visitors when Natasha arrived, so she took the time to walk around the museum once more by herself. She walked the length of the wall again, noticing that she'd met some of the people who had sent notes. John and Rose. Linda and Jocelyn. Mark, Kevin, and their young daughter Chloe.

All of these stories were enough for a book rather than one article. She'd have to see what Anna thought of the latest draft she sent her. Perhaps there was room for a follow-up?

"Natasha, thank you so much for waiting."

"It's no problem. After all I came here to ask a favor of you."

"And I'm happy to make time for you now. What more would you like to know?"

Natasha looked back at the wall. "Can we stay here for a moment?"

"Sure."

"All right. I met a lot of people yesterday, and generally during my time here in Pinedale. There are so many stories...and they all seem to believe that the Christmas Cupid is a real thing. People come here and fall in love."

"You sound like you still haven't made up your mind."

"Would you mind a personal question?"

"Not at all, go ahead," Marilyn said without hesitation.

"Okay. I imagine you've seen a lot of pictures being added to the wall, and many people returning for Ivy's Christmas. Isn't it hard for you?"

"Why would it be? I'm surrounded by love and holiday cheer. The way my husband and I loved it, and the way he would want it for me..." Marilyn let her words trail off as if she understood the deeper meaning of Natasha's question. Maybe she did. "I won't lie to you, it's hard sometimes, and I miss him every day. But it would have been worse to miss out on a single moment we had together."

"It's not triggering for you when people come together over the story?"

"I'm not sure I'd use that word. It all brings me back, and I welcome that. At the same time, I'm in the present, and I have lovely people in my life, like Ivy. Fate gives us opportunities. That's all. We shouldn't take them for granted, but no one can say we can't celebrate them."

"It all changes," Natasha said wistfully.

"You used to love Christmas."

"Don't we all, at some point?" She had no intention of explaining to Marilyn what had cemented her conviction that it was all a pretense, often stressful and expensive.

"Look, you're right about this—part of it is a story, a legend, and people stay or come back here time after time to celebrate it. They know that life can be hard and throw you curveballs. But that's not the point. They chose love and light, and no matter how tough it gets, they'll always have that. I have that, and you do too."

Self-conscious, Natasha laughed. "How do you know?" All of a sudden excited, she almost expected Marilyn to name the matchmaker herself. Marilyn's answer surprised her.

"Someone who cares about you sent you to Pinedale. And you came here and are making friends at every turn. That's something, isn't it?"

Friends. Okay.

"I guess I have more of a social life here than I've had in months. That's also because it's so small, you can't help stumbling across the same people."

"And those people like to spend time with you and talk to you. I hope you remember that when you go home."

"Oh, I'll remember all of you," Natasha promised. "Everyone of you has been extremely helpful."

"Thank you. We can always use a few more visitors to discover our town. Will you come back next year?"

"Me?" *I wasn't even invited to the party.* How long was she going to sulk about that? "I'm not sure I should. After all it's for people who...You know what? Thank you so much, Marilyn, but I think I should go. I forgot something."

Marilyn gave her a knowing smile.

"That sounds important. Good luck."

"Thank you." She might need it. Did good luck override fate? Was it one and the same? When she left the museum, Natasha could see kids waiting in line for Santa at the toy store. She heard voices sing somewhere, realizing they came from the steps of the church where a choir had assembled.

Yes, there had been a time when she'd loved Christmas, couldn't wait for it to arrive. For a long time afterwards, that period had felt empty and dark, until she had a well-paying job and decided she deserved warmth and sunlight.

The latter was already disappearing once more, but Natasha hadn't lacked warmth since she'd arrived in Pinedale. She hurried the few steps along to the bakery, hoping it was still open. Ivy stood outside in her coat, listening to the song with a soft smile on her face.

God Rest Ye Merry Gentlemen.

"Are you going home?" Natasha asked.

"Not yet. I just came outside for a moment, because...It's hot in the kitchen, and I like listening to them."

So they did, for a few minutes and a couple of more songs.

"You'd like to come in?"

"Yes, no...I..." Why was she at a loss for words all of a sudden? "You know I'm going home soon."

"Yes." Ivy lowered her gaze, studying the tips of her boots.

"And I said I'd help you with the tree. Whenever you're ready, I'll be there." She couldn't blame Ivy for the surprise in her expression when she looked up.

"I know I ran out on you the other day. I'm sorry."

"Come in for a moment?"

In the café, there were still a few patrons, families and couples. One of the latter...She couldn't believe her eyes. There was Lara with a man. The two of them were holding hands, gazing deep into each other's eyes.

"You've got to be kidding me," she couldn't hold back the comment.

"I'm not. That was so quick, it surprised even me. I think I'll invite both of them to the party." After a small pause, she added. "I would have invited you, but you won't be here."

"No. I'm sorry."

Natasha truly was, feeling like that chance had just slipped through her fingers. What was she hoping for? That they would have kissed under the mistletoe?

She held Ivy's gaze, all of a sudden unable to look away.

Ivy broke the spell first, turning away before she waved to Mark and Kevin. "I'll be right there. I'm sorry, but can you wait? They ordered something to go."

"Yes, sure, no problem."

Jessie and Alina were sitting in a booth, sharing a kiss.

Bridget and her husband.

Lara...she wasn't the one for the Christmas Cupid.

It didn't work that way.

Natasha felt a bit silly, but she couldn't help smiling at the realization.

Chapter Thirteen

IVY

S he loved making everyone happy by being a gracious host, sharing many delicacies...Today, Ivy couldn't wait until the last customer had left the café. She still did most of the cleaning up herself with her staff. She never was in much of a hurry, until today. To her dismay, it must have shown, because Tina told her, "Please, go. We can finish up the rest. I can open tomorrow morning if you like."

"No, that's fine. I'll be here." She had to. Come to the bakery first thing in the morning—what other people would still call night—start everything by herself, Ivy had to do it. It had to be done this way. There could be no deviation. "I might take you up on the other offer though. Are you sure it's not too much?"

"Come on, Ivy. You always stay longer than anyone, and you come here every day before us. Have some fun."

She blushed hotly, unsure whether Tina was referring to Natasha waiting for her in the café. Dinner. They'd have to get something for dinner before or after finishing the tree. Natasha loved the *Baumkuchen*, so that's what dessert would be.

"Okay, thank you so much. I'll make it up to you."

"No need. If I can take home a few of those *Vanillekipferl* too?"

In Ivy's opinion, Tina, who had been working at her side for the third year in a row, deserved more than the vanilla crescent cookies, but she'd come back to that.

"Of course. Enjoy."

"You know I will."

Natasha was still working on her laptop when Ivy returned but closed it as soon as she saw her.

"I think that's enough for me too, at least for today. Let's put some decorations on that tree."

"I can't wait. Though...would you like to have dinner first?" She couldn't believe how awkward and shy she sounded, like asking out a girl for the first time. Come to think of it, that was exactly like she'd sounded that day. Ivy shook the memory. She was a grown woman now, a business owner. She was having dinner with...a friend. A friend she'd grown close to over the past few days, closer than she usually allowed herself.

"I'd love to. Betty's? Though I'm not sure I'll be able to move after one of those plates."

"I was thinking we could go to my place? Eat, and then decorate the tree?"

"Sounds great to me," was Natasha's swift answer.

"Okay. Let's do it then. It's not far. We could walk, but I brought my car this morning, so..."

"It's fine," Natasha stopped her, sounding amused. "I have time. I'm only waiting for feedback from my boss now." She winced a little as if she had anything to worry about. Ivy had since learned that Natasha was one of *East Coast Magazine*'s most acclaimed writers.

"I still wish you could stay. But we'll have a nice evening anyway."

The only answer she got this time was a smile full of promise. Ivy hoped she'd be calm enough to drive.

Once they were in the car, she turned on the radio, the song *My Grown-Up Christmas List* playing. "Is that okay with you?"

"Perfect," Natasha confirmed.

During the drive, Ivy tried to remember when she'd last gone grocery shopping, and if there was anything in her fridge or pantry that would work for a quick, but also impressive dinner. She would have to improvise which was so different from her day job, where precision was key, and she couldn't just substitute one ingredient for another.

She ruefully admitted that this was an excellent metaphor for her life. Things had to stay a certain way. Messing with the chemistry of it all could lead to potentially disastrous consequences. Except right now, the chemistry felt just fine.

"I hope you don't expect too much," she told Natasha. "I'm a decent baker, but my cooking skills are fairly basic."

"Don't worry. I'm sure we can throw something together."

We. "I invited you."

"And I offered to help. I don't often have the opportunity to cook, but I like it. I promise you we'll be fine."

Natasha had gone from pensive to decidedly optimistic. Ivy didn't mind being along for the ride. She'd have enough reflection on New Year's Eve and New Year's Day.

The time for cheer was just beginning, and for some reason, she felt more cheerful than ever.

It hadn't snowed in a couple of days, but the hills were glistening white in the distance. To Ivy, this was the perfect home, not too far from the bakery, but far enough that she could enjoy a bit of solitude as well. She noticed Natasha's curious expression.

"This was my parents' house. I grew up here."

Her heart skipped a beat at the undisguised affection in Natasha's smile.

"I keep learning new things about you."

"I have to keep some of the suspense...No, that's not the reason. I'm just not used to revealing so much about myself in such a short time."

"I can relate to that," Natasha admitted. "Pinedale has a way of bringing out those stories."

"It sure has."

"Would it be too nosy to ask why your parents moved out of Pinedale?"

"Not at all. My Dad got sick...he's fine now," she hurried to say. "But they needed to be closer to the clinic at the time. They started by renting a house."

"That must have been difficult," Natasha said.

"At first, yes," Ivy admitted. "Fortunately, Dad got better. Then they got the chance to buy their now home, and they went for it, and signed this one over to me. They like where they are, but they still talk about coming back here one day."

This was a shorter, simplified version of the story. Ivy thought it was enough for the evening.

"I imagine it would be hard to keep a low profile for anyone from your family."

"I don't think they worry about that. There's just a time for everything, right? I knew when it was time for me to come here and re-open the bakery. But now we should be thinking of dinner first, then I'll get the decorations from the attic."

"Sure."

Natasha followed her into the kitchen where Ivy opened doors of pantry and fridge, hoping to look like someone who had a plan. She took out peppers and onions, and a bottle of red wine.

"Would you like to start with this?"

Natasha laughed. "Dangerous, but I won't say no."

She had no idea how much this summed up Ivy's whole experience with her.

·♥·♥·♥·♥·♥·

With the second glass, they had a chicken skillet dinner with vegetables and rice which wasn't half bad. Ivy wanted to ask some fairly nosy questions too, though she wasn't sure if it was her place to do so. Natasha seemed relaxed and happy, and perhaps she shouldn't question any of it. Ivy was aware of her own state of mind.

Being here with her, having a meal with Christmas music playing in the background, it felt like home. More than Ivy had ever experienced home in her adult life.

It meant something. She couldn't afford to dwell on it though.

Natasha's place was somewhere else. Ivy's place was here in Pinedale, celebrating the holidays with everyone who came to value love over everything else.

Sometimes, being Cupid could be a blessing and a curse.

"I'm sure you're wondering why there are next to no decorations in the house," she said. "I'm cutting it close as usual. We always used to put out the advent wreath," she pointed to the centerpiece on the coffee table, a wreath from pine branches with decorations and four candles. "I start with that, and then work takes over."

"It's beautiful," Natasha said. "We have time for the rest now. Where do we start?"

"I've got some boxes in the attic, and the tree's on the back porch."

"All right, let's do this."

97

A pull-down ladder gave access to the attic space. Ivy went up to get the boxes, and Natasha stayed down to receive them and bring them to the living room. Her eyes widened when she realized how many there were.

"You didn't really expect anything else from me, did you?" Ivy asked, laughing.

"Come to think of it, no, not really."

"The heavy one has the stand for the tree." Ivy bent to take it out and took a critical look around. Usually I put it here, by the fireplace."

"Perfect choice. When did you get the tree?"

"Oh, I didn't. Every year, someone in town drops it off at my back porch. I never know who it comes from, and they don't expect anything in return. I just pay it forward..."

"With the Christmas lottery. Wait, that's not a real thing?" Natasha asked, baffled, when Ivy didn't answer right away.

"No, not really," Ivy admitted. "We have a day, though, when all the baking goes to the shelter."

Shaking her head, Natasha said, "I used to think it was just the Cupid story that was unbelievable. This town is like a dream."

"I know what you mean. Like you feel you have to tread carefully, or you're going to wake up from it?"

Natasha held her gaze for a long moment. "Exactly like that."

Chapter Fourteen

NATASHA

With some wriggling and lots of laughter they got the tree in its place. The scent of its needles was irreversibly associated with bittersweet memories she hadn't dared to confront in years. She could almost hear the sound of wrapping paper being torn by small hands eager to get to the presents Santa had brought. Lights sparkling and reflecting in fragile decorations, adults exchanging happy glances. Fragile was all that had remained.

Natasha's thoughts wandered back to her conversation with Marilyn.

Anna had little knowledge about Natasha's perspective on Christmas, other that she took the time off and sent cards that had beaches and turquoise water on them. Did she guess? Did she care? Was that why she had sent Natasha here?

In any case, she should go and get some Pinedale postcards to send home.

With the fir standing tall, she and Ivy got started on the lights, and the decorations after that. A lot of them were the classic round shape, made from glass, in red, gold and other colors.

"Is there any particular order?" she asked.

"No, just put them where there's room."

Natasha remembered all of it, carefully reaching out to place item after item on the tree, everything that was in those boxes, the more the better.

She and Ivy worked silently side by side, both of them, Natasha assumed, lost in memories. Not completely lost. She was grateful for the woman next to her, anchoring her in the present, reminding her that she was an adult able to make choices.

She could be cynical about all of it if she wanted to.

She could let herself enjoy the warmth and the lights. It didn't mean she was gullible or naïve, as long as it was her choice to believe that dreams could come true at Christmas. Natasha turned to Ivy wondering what would happen if she made that particular dream come true...

It wasn't fair, she decided. They could have fun, be friends, and enjoy the time they could spend together because a coincidence had brought them here. She'd help Ivy with her website if or when that became a subject. It was all she could do.

Ivy took a half step closer, and Natasha stepped back, bending to take out the tree topper, a serene-looking angel. Did every family have one of those?

"Here," she said, handing it to Ivy. "You want to do the honors?"

"Thank you." Ivy's smile was tinged with an emotion Natasha was wrestling with as well. But if they went too far, disappointment and regret would be worse. They had to keep it as merry as possible—that was the story. She went up the ladder to put the angel on top, then came down and folded it.

"Let's just put this away, and I'll get us the dessert I promised."

The empty boxes went back up the attic, and after putting the ladder away, Ivy went to make coffee.

Natasha walked around the room that was now full of light. From the fireplace, the tree, and other decorations they'd put up. Outside, big snowflakes had started to fall, the landscape looking soft and quiet.

It had been a long time since she'd experienced this, slowing down to enjoy the season instead of being around people who got more stressed and tense every minute.

On her previous vacations, she had tried her best to relax. Even in those places, Natasha had been aware of people joining every excursion, attending every event the hotel offered, trying to fill every minute of the day.

She couldn't help wondering what they were trying to avoid. Afraid to admit they had fallen for someone? Feeling silly because they wanted to kiss them, but had stepped back at the last moment? That would be her.

Natasha stood by the window, watching the snow fall, the lights of another town far in the distance—startled when she realized she wished she didn't have to leave. But even if she stayed over the holidays, where could they go from there? Ivy had a job to return to, and so did Natasha.

Before going to sleep tonight, she'd browse some of those last-minute vacation websites. They had been her friend for the past few years. They'd come through for her again.

Ivy returned to the living room with a tray holding two cups of hot chocolate, and Natasha's favorite, the *Baumkuchen*, thin layers of cake and a dark chocolate ganache.

"Let's sit for a moment," she said. "Thank you for doing this with me."

Given the weather and the time of day, Natasha should have left, but that would make her a terrible guest.

"Any time. It was fun."

"Yes. I think my family was always the last one to put up the tree, because that's how they did it...For me, it's mostly because I'm always running out of time."

"But we made it."

"Yes, we made it." Ivy gazed at the lights on the tree, the sparkle reflected in her eyes. She was beautiful.

Natasha directed her focus on the sweet offerings. "I love this cake," she said. "Did I mention I'll have to bring home a ton? Perhaps I should have you send it."

"You didn't say a ton, but yes, you mentioned it. I'll send it to you, no problem."

"This was nice. I haven't decorated a tree since I was a kid."

Ivy didn't say anything, but the question was clear in her expression. For a long time, Natasha had felt like the story was something she should be embarrassed about, because she'd fallen for a ruse. It was easy to see now why she had resisted believing another story that sounded too good to be true...that could end up in hurting those who invested too much in it.

"It is a bit of a sad story, but please don't pity me, okay?"

It might be the generous amount of Grand Marnier in the hot chocolate that paved the path to more revelations—but so be it. Soon enough, Natasha would pick up her life far from Pinedale and Ivy. She wasn't so easily rattled at other times of the year.

"I'm the last one who could pity anyone. We do what feels right, and safe."

"I guess. It's really fascinating, everywhere I go and ask questions, people ask me questions in return—and I would normally draw the line. I'm the writer after all. But Marilyn reminded me of when I last loved Christmas. I used to believe it was real, the magic, that everything was possible." She had Ivy's full attention which Natasha found both disconcerting and reassuring. Either way she couldn't back out now. "I could tell that things had been tense between my parents for a while. They knew something I didn't, so they wanted to make sure that Christmas would be the most amazing...and at the time, it was. Decorations, food, gifts, everything was over the top. They didn't fight at all that night."

Ivy waited patiently as Natasha continued.

"We went to church on Christmas Eve, had a huge brunch the next day, went for a sleigh ride...Like every year, we got that cherry pie I loved from a local diner. Lots of cream," she remembered, unable to keep the smile off her face.

"It sounds like a dream."

"Right." Only when Ivy winced, Natasha realized her tone had hardened. She sighed. "By New Year's Eve, I found out that's all it was. Dad moved out in January, and he remarried a few years later. I don't think Mom ever got over it, but the following years, they tried to outdo one another. Christmas became a competition." No one at work, or the friends she'd made since leaving college, knew this. Why did the words come tumbling out now?

Pinedale.

"Anyway, Mom got sick, and after she passed away, I never really went back. Dad and I send Christmas cards, and we call on birthdays. That's the story."

"I'm sorry," Ivy said, sounding genuine.

Natasha sensed she had more questions. They might be the same she had tried to answer for herself, without success.

"Thank you. I guess looking back, it all makes sense. Of course, Christmas is great for children, when you don't know what cost and effort it takes to make it all happen. You just see the shine…I used to love the holidays, but I could never find out when the pretense started."

"So to be on the safe side, you accepted the idea that nothing was real?"

"Something like that."

Ivy looked troubled. "It must have been so hard to find out, but don't you think they tried because they loved you most of all? I'm not saying the competition is a great thing, but perhaps it was less for them than it was an attempt to distract you, make you happy?"

"See, that's exactly the problem. I can't stand lies and pretense. It's better to know."

"And now? Do you know?"

Before Natasha had a chance to respond, Ivy leaned forward and hugged her. As much as she had other ideas not long ago, she leaned into the much-needed embrace.

"I don't pretend for anyone's sake," Ivy whispered. "I try my best to create cookies and opportunities for people, and they do the rest. I'm terrible at making it happen for myself, but I'm so glad I met you. I like you."

Holding her felt much like it had in Natasha's dream, but things had been vague and a bit blurry. She could see clearly now.

Natasha pulled back, holding Ivy's gaze for a moment before she leaned in to kiss her softly, tasting the chocolate on her lips. No, there was no pretense.

It was all true.

Chapter Fifteen

IVY

In the past few hours, she had sensed that the moment would come, and she'd been afraid the aftermath might be awkward, uncomfortable. Instead, the world around them and inside them was calm.

The pieces were falling into place, one by one. Their experiences growing up had shaped them, but in the present, they were adults, responsible for their own lives...and happiness. Sharing those memories only served to make them more aware, conscious of their choices.

Regardless of the fact that there was no way Natasha would get a cab at this time of night, or that Ivy would have to be up in a few hours, they sat huddled together on the couch, under the soft comforter.

"Call me crazy," Natasha said, "This is already the best Christmas I've had in many years."

Ivy turned to her, just to make sure she wasn't dreaming, and their lips met again.

"For me too."

"You're saying in all those years, no one's ever fallen for the Christmas Cupid? I find that hard to believe," Natasha teased her.

"Right. Like you find other things hard to believe, but it's true. I'm sort of their mascot. A mediator if you will, but they don't consider me relationship material." Was she getting far ahead of herself? They hadn't been talking about a relationship.

And even if they never did, Ivy wouldn't regret those kisses. There might be another cupid in town, because she knew she'd been hit.

"Then they couldn't see what was right in front of them."

Natasha didn't elaborate, and they sat in silence, watching the hypnotic dance of the flames in the fireplace until it lulled them to sleep.

NATASHA

B olting upright when her phone woke her, Natasha felt disoriented for a few seconds before she turned off the offending sound and assured herself that next to her, Ivy was still asleep. In the fireplace, the fire had gone out, but the lights and soft music were still on.

The snow was still falling.

3:37 a.m. It wouldn't be long until Ivy had to get up and go to the bakery. Natasha decided to stay—nothing awkward or uncomfortable about what happened. They'd decorated a tree, shared some family secrets and fallen asleep on the couch after...The memories of those kisses made her face flush with excitement. All of a sudden, there was an added layer of thrill to her time in Pinedale, though she regretted having to cut it short.

She looked at her phone again, realizing Anna had sent a series of text messages, with a couple of voicemails in between.

I knew you had it in you. A bit cheesy, but that's what we were going for. Still reads you between the lines.

Good job. Now answer the phone!

I know you're enjoying the baked goods, but I need you to be here for the meeting on the 24th. Please confirm.

Natasha made a face. In the past, if she wasn't already lounging in the beach, she didn't mind coming in on the 24th. Sometimes she had brought a suitcase and gone straight to the airport from there...She shook her head at her thoughts. Why would she mind this year? If she didn't go to the meeting, she'd be home alone, in an apartment where nothing reminded her of the holidays. She had always known that once Anna approved the article, she'd have to go back, and that it would be before Christmas. She had put off booking that flight for obvious reasons, but she couldn't wait any longer.

Thanks. I'll be there, she texted back.

When she put away her phone, Natasha realized that Ivy was watching her.

"Is there a problem?"

"No, nothing. I'm sorry if this woke you."

"No problem." Ivy yawned. "I have to get ready anyway. If you'd like, you could have a shower here and we have breakfast at the bakery? I could also drop you off at the B&B if you prefer."

"I can get all the sleep I want once I'm back home." Natasha didn't want to reveal that the day would come sooner than later, but she didn't have much of a choice. "I think I'll take you up on the first offer, and I'll hang out at the bakery a bit longer, finish up some things."

"Great. You heard from your boss?"

"Yes. She's scheduled a meeting for the 24th."

"On Christmas Eve?"

Maybe Ivy, too, had hoped that Natasha had changed her plans. She might have, if it wasn't for Anna's message.

"Yeah. But everything going as planned so far. I'm certain this will put you further on the map out of state. And Pinedale."

Natasha wished she could be here for it. The party—and beyond.

"I can't thank you enough. This means a lot." A hesitant smile showed Natasha that perhaps she wasn't just talking about the opportunities for her business.

"I'm happy to help. Now let's get started, because for some completely inexplicable reason I'm ready to eat again."

Ivy was laughing as she walked out of the room.

Natasha looked around, and with a sigh, went to turn off the lights and the radio.

Every time she was truly at peace, it ended too soon.

.♥ . ♥ . ♥ . ♥ . ♥ .

Ivy made time for a quick coffee and breakfast with rolls she served with jams, cheese, and cold cuts. After that, she left Natasha to her own devices once again.

She started by sending a *Merry Christmas* email to one of her colleagues, a graphic designer, and asked her if she'd be willing to help with a potential online store.

Next...With a sigh she opened the airline's website, starting the search for flights. Pinedale didn't have an airport, but even considering she would have to take a cab, it would be faster than taking the scenic train ride again.

She couldn't help but shudder. Somehow, here in Pinedale she got used to being up early, but traveling in the middle of the night wasn't something she looked forward to. Especially since she wasn't looking forward to leaving at all. Natasha opened another tab and typed in *Caribbean Last Minute*. If she attended the meeting on the 24th, worked another couple of days, she could be in Cancun, Aruba or Turks and Caicos before New Year's Eve. She might even save a few bucks since Christmas wasn't included.

The million-dollar question: Did she still want to go?

Natasha closed the tab and continued sipping her coffee.

Having to go back wasn't an option. Being alone wasn't. So why wouldn't she make it as comfortable as possible?

"You need anything else? A refill?"

She nearly dropped her cup at the sound of Ivy's voice, as if she'd done something forbidden.

"No, thank you, I'm fine."

"Are you sure?"

No, I'm not. But I put myself in this situation, and I have to deal with it.

"I swear, it's all good. We're good. I've been looking at flights."

"I see. Be sure to check the weather forecast. There's a lot more snow coming, and there might be delays."

"Thanks, I will." She wanted to say so much more, but an employee came over to ask Ivy a question, and Natasha reminded herself that Ivy had more important things to tend to.

Chapter Sixteen

IVY

No matter her own emotional turmoil, there was still a ton of *Lebkuchen* and other tasty Christmas treats to bake.

Ivy was exhausted, which wasn't such a surprise as they were getting closer to Christmas. Today, she would have loved to close the bakery and stay in, have some more time with Natasha, just to talk about whether they had any future beyond Pinedale, and what that would look like.

Or perhaps sleep some more. The couch was comfortable, and it had been even lovelier to share it with Natasha, but it wasn't the best for her back. She was anxious. She needed to get over herself and serve her customers as always. The day after tomorrow, she had to deliver baked goods to the Christmas party.

Thanks to Natasha, her own house was all decked out for the holidays now...She cast a look at the industrial oven. Only a few hundred more cookies to go. Piece of cake.

"Are you okay?" Tina asked. "If you'd like to take a break..."

"Thank you, but no. We still have a lot of work to do."

"Sure, boss."

Ivy made it out to the counter in time to greet Linda and Jocelyn who were coming in, their coats and hats coated in thick snow.

"Wow, it's really coming down now," Linda said. "But there's nothing keeping us away from our afternoon snack when you're in town."

Ivy gave her a tired smile, an idea springing to mind. What if...? She quickly pushed the thought aside. There was no way she could be so lucky. Her mission was to bring luck and love to others.

She had no power over road conditions and such, and it wouldn't be kind to hope for circumstances that would keep Natasha in Pinedale. She really needed that sleep.

"And I see Natasha keeps coming back too," Jocelyn observed, sharing a look with her wife.

"She's finishing up her work here. Looking for a flight home actually." Ivy hoped her disappointment didn't come through, but she wasn't that lucky.

"Why doesn't she stay over the holidays, go back after Christmas at least? She can send her work via email?"

Ivy cast a glance over at where Natasha sat frowning at the screen of her laptop.

"It seems she has to be there in person."

"And after that?"

"Come on. I'm leaving after Valentine's Day."

"Yeah, so?" Jocelyn wasn't ready to give up. "It's not that long. You have something planned together?"

"Jo." Linda's tone held a note of both affection and warning. "I don't think it's any of our business what the two have planned."

Why would they even think that?

Perhaps what she had refused to acknowledge, pushed away until Natasha kissed her, had been obvious to everyone else.

Christmas was only a couple of days away.

Ivy was in love.

And all of a sudden, she knew she couldn't let Natasha leave without knowing that there was a plan.

"Excuse me," she said.

Ivy headed over to the table where Natasha was about to pack up. "Please, wait."

It sounded urgent enough.

"I know you're pretty busy as always, but perhaps we could have dinner at Betty's again."

"No, I mean...Yes, I'd like that, but I need to tell you something." Realizing that some of the patrons had taken an interest in their conversation, Ivy lowered her voice. "I understand that you have to miss the party, because you'll have to go back to your work and all, but I need something from you."

"Anything," Natasha said, not taking her eyes off Ivy. "Can you sit for a moment?"

Ivy looked back at the counter where two of her employees were handling the line, handing bags and packages to customers. Some came for the big basket she offered during the last few days before Christmas.

"Not really. Not yet. But before you go, I need to know if I'm silly, and fooling myself, or if there's a chance we'll see each other after this."

"I told you I hate lies, so I won't lie to you." Natasha's tone was serious. "I want to. I'm not sure if and how we can make it work, but I want to see you again."

"Okay. Good." Ivy took a deep breath. "That's all I need for now."

Natasha reached out to take her hand which seemed to cause a collective sigh in the room.

"Are you sure everything is okay?"

"Yes. I'm just tired. I'll see you later at Betty's?"

"You definitely will."

Ivy was still exhausted, but the rest of her workday felt a little less heavy—even though Natasha hadn't promised anything definitive.

She hoped she wasn't going at this all wrong, jinxing any chance she might have. She had to do something. They were running out of time.

Ivy couldn't forget about all the other people that counted on her, year after year.

This time, she'd find a moment to take care of her own dreams and hopes as well, wherever that might lead.

NATASHA

As she was getting ready for her dinner with Ivy, her nervousness rose with each minute. Once upon a time, Natasha's life had been a set of comfortable patterns, not all of them functional, but comfortable.

She didn't do Christmas, because it was all a stressful, expensive scam.

She didn't do second dates because...well, the reason was pretty much the same.

Natasha would still come home to an empty, distinctively Christmas-free apartment. As for the other subject, it was hard to say when to even start counting. Their earlier dinners or meals shared throughout long days, kisses after decorating the tree, falling asleep next to each other on Ivy's couch?

By all measures, tonight was a real date, and Ivy was right to say they needed to have a plan. Natasha wasn't averse to plans as they took away much of the scary, unexpected. But how would this work? They lived two states away from each other. The bakery might work four months a year. Natasha wasn't sure a relationship could, and her revolving thoughts made her irritated and antsy.

Still, she couldn't help smiling when Ivy knocked on the door of her room, and instead of hello, Natasha pulled her close for a kiss. She was almost ready to suggest they'd skip Betty's and get a snack somewhere later...

She didn't want to make life any more complicated, for her or Ivy.

"You're ready?" Ivy asked, her earlier worries seemingly forgotten. In Pinedale, people understood how to live in the moment, another lesson that Natasha could benefit from.

"I am. Let's go."

The snowfall was still heavy, but since Betty's was only a few blocks away, they went on foot. Children were having a snowball fight on the front lawn of a family home. They walked by as the mom called them inside for dinner, and caught a glimpse of a decorated hallway.

Natasha remembered thinking so many times that people would put themselves into debt with the electricity bills that would wait for them after the holidays. Now all she could see was the sparkle in the children's eyes.

She'd once taken in the world with a sense of wonder. Was it really all gone? Who was to say? If she'd been happy, and that was her parents' goal, why would she doubt that?

She cast a glance at Ivy, whose reaction was an easy, warm smile. Maybe Natasha had never lost that wonder, just tucked it away safely for a while—a long while—waiting for someone to bring it back.

Someone to love—to love her.

Before she could let the words tumble out, they had arrived, and Ivy held the door of Betty's open to her.

Once they got out of their coats and found a place, Natasha began, "So I'm going to leave tomorrow morning so I can be there for the meeting. Anna wants everyone there in person."

"Okay."

Ivy was giving her every chance, every opportunity to get this right. The problem was Natasha wasn't sure what the right thing to do was. According to her initial plan, she would have booked her vacation the moment she left the meeting.

Ivy would be here for a little while longer, busy, though probably not as much as before Christmas?

"I'm not sure what will happen after that. What you would like to happen," she added quickly. "You'll still be here until the end of February?"

"As every year," Ivy confirmed. "Usually, I go straight back home and to my job. I have an arrangement but being gone as long as I am each year, I can't stretch it much more."

"I understand. I guess what I'm saying is...What are you doing on New Year's Eve?"

It was one of the songs that had played on the radio while they were falling asleep together.

"You could be back here so soon?" Ivy's eyes lit up as if she hadn't even considered that possibility.

"It looks like Anna is happy with the story now, so I can't imagine she wouldn't give me a few days."

"That would be wonderful. It will still be a bit crazy, but not as much."

"We could figure it out. I think in the past few days, we've had a lot of work and cheer, and very little sleep."

"No kidding," Ivy admitted ruefully.

"So, we're doing this? Ringing in the New Year together?"

"We will. I can't wait."

"Don't be too impatient. First of all, you'll be celebrating Christmas with all those wonderful people who helped us see the light." Natasha couldn't help laughing at her wording. "Listen to me. The Grinch has come to her senses."

"I always knew you had a big heart," Ivy said.

Later, Natasha would barely remember what she ate, but she'd always remember that moment between them, promising more than either of them had imagined for themselves.

·♥·♥·♥·♥·♥·

She had managed to book a flight that didn't require her to get up at 2:00 a.m., but Natasha was glad she had called the cab early when she stepped onto the sidewalk and her boots sank into the fresh snow.

There were so many ways she'd rather spent the day, but she hadn't forgotten Anna's warnings about layoffs. Aside from that, Natasha was invested in a successful outcome for Ivy. She might have risked skipping the meeting—ironically, she couldn't do it, because for their plans, the story as well as Natasha having an income in the future, mattered. She'd come back with an even lighter heart knowing Anna signed off on the latest version and would still employ Natasha in the future.

Fortunately, the driver didn't try to make small talk, so she leaned back and closed her eyes. When she opened them again, Natasha was startled to realize that while they weren't anywhere near the airport, they were almost standing still.

"What's happening?" she asked.

The driver shrugged. "Winter?"

"I can see that. You think you can still make it to the airport in time?" She had planned a bigger window, but if they were moving at this pace, she might still be late.

This wasn't possible. Everything had to work according to schedule from now on, and she couldn't be late or miss the meeting. Missing the meeting and the Christmas party? No way.

"I'm sorry, Ma'am, but I'm not making that call."

"I know. I'm sorry too." She leaned back into the seat with a sigh, acknowledging it was better going nowhere safely than causing harm.

Chapter Seventeen

IVY

Natasha was probably about to board her plane. Ivy had been on her feet since the alarm had rung at the usual time, baking, decorating, and filling in everywhere.

Christmas Eve always saw one of the biggest crowds during the season, people picking up their orders, needing a last-minute present or deciding on a snack on the whim of the moment.

Even though the weather conditions brought fewer of the latter into the *Magic Christmas Bakery*, the café was once again full, and the line stretching out onto the sidewalk.

No matter how tired she was, Ivy never failed to keep a smile on her face. She had so much to be happy and grateful for—her family, her friends, and Natasha who had quickly become both to her. She'd be back for New Year's Eve.

Amazing things were in her future. Who said the Christmas Cupid couldn't find love where everyone else had? They were going to tell a whole new story. She might not be happy that Natasha's boss was ordering her back, but she had to thank her for sending her in the first place. This article was going to change everything, and not just because it meant even more customers.

At 1:00 p.m. she finally closed behind the last patron, a gust of wind driving snow inside when she held the door open for the woman with the many bags.

"I'll see you later at the party?"

Ivy was so tired she almost hadn't recognized Bridget.

"Of course. Just don't worry if I fall asleep."

Bridget laughed. "Good to know in advance. Just relax a bit. Let someone else get you something sweet."

"I'll try. See you."

Ivy locked the door, taking a deep breath. After she, Tina and another employee had cleaned up, she'd pack up a few boxes.

No matter how many times she told herself that everything was going according to plan, she still wished that Natasha could have stayed.

·♥·♥·♥·♥·♥·

"Okay, that was the last one," Tina said, closing the trunk after they'd carried box after box to Ivy's car. "Are you sure you don't need any help?"

"Oh no, thank you. It's all set up. I'll just get these over to the museum, and head home to change. I hope everyone remembers what they offered to bring."

Tina laughed. "I'm sure Alina and Jessie were thorough about that. I'll see you later, then. It's a good thing you don't live that far."

"That's why everyone has four-wheel drive in Pinedale. You'll pick up Marilyn?"

"Of course. I can't wait."

"Me neither," Ivy said. She was truly looking forward to having all of her Pinedale friends in one place, though that hint of melancholy hadn't gone unnoticed by Tina.

"It's a shame Natasha couldn't make it. Next year?"

"Yes. I hope."

They went their separate ways, and Ivy sat inside her car. She hoped Natasha had made it to her destination, not stuck on the road or in an airport somewhere.

She'd arrived in Pinedale by train, but on holidays they didn't depart as early as she'd needed.

Ivy took out her phone and texted, *Stay safe and let me know when you arrive. Can't wait for you to be back. Merry Christmas.*

There was more in her heart, but everything between them was still so new and fragile, it would be a mistake to get ahead of herself. Ivy started her car and made her way to the museum. Even the short drive took longer than usual, the reduced visibility slowing down traffic.

When she arrived at the museum, Ivy had a hard time trusting her eyes. A truck was crowding the small parking lot, and the doors of the building stood wide open. Near the entrance, Marilyn stood with Alina, Jessie and a man in coveralls.

When they saw Ivy, Marilyn came heading towards her.

"What happened? I just came to drop off the cakes..."

"Oh Ivy." The older woman's eyes brimmed with unshed tears. "I'm afraid we need to call off the party. A pipe burst on the upper floor, and there's been some water damage. There's no way we can clean all of that up in time, and with the number of people coming, we need running water..."

Ivy's heart sank, and not just because of the food in her trunk,

"But...the pictures and notes. Is it all destroyed?" She, too, was barely blinking back tears. This couldn't happen, not ever, and not this year of all years.

She feared the worst when Marilyn reached out to touch her shoulder.

"We were able to save them."

"Thank God," was the only thing Ivy could think of. She still felt light-headed. Those stories were a big part of Pinedale's history.

"We were very lucky," Marilyn agreed.

"Hey, Ivy." Jessie had joined them. "It's true that we were lucky, but what are we going to do now? I think we have to call everyone."

"Wait. No. I mean, yes, call them, but we're going to have a party." Ivy wasn't going to give up so easily now that the worst was averted. "We'll do it at my house."

Marilyn's eyes widened. "You'd do that? You must have been on your feet for twenty-four hours straight."

"Almost, but it doesn't matter. Everyone brings over their food. Maybe you'll just put a sign at the door?"

"We can bring the dishes, utensils, and napkins," Jessie offered. "And a few extra chairs."

"Good. I'll handle everything else. Just make sure everybody gets over there slowly and safely."

Jessie and Marilyn shared a surprised smile, then Jessie pulled her into a quick firm hug.

"Thanks, Cupid. We can always count on you to make Christmas perfect."

Ivy was determined to live up to that promise. As she headed back to her car, she couldn't help wishing that she could do the same for Natasha.

First, she had a lot to do.

· ♥ · ♥ · ♥ · ♥ ·

She spent the next half hour on her commute, twice the time she usually needed.

Ivy brought all the boxes full of delicacies into her home, careful not to slip on the fresh snow. Closing the front door behind her, she realized that her hat, gloves and scarf were wet. She sighed in relief after taking them off.

A quick hot shower and changing into clothes more appropriate for the evening were next on the agenda, then she started to set up tables and chairs.

Ivy brought down some folding chairs from the attic. Together with the seating in her living room, some dining room chairs, and the ones Jessie and Alina were bringing, they should be fine. She took tablecloths she hadn't used in years, out of drawers, and placed some of her own dishes and utensils on the table. The weather and changed location might make a difference, but Ivy couldn't think of a Christmas party in Pinedale that didn't come with a few surprise guests.

In the living room, Ivy cast a fond glance at the tree and other decorations that had transformed the space. She fervently hoped that next year, she and Natasha would be able to spend Christmas together. Thank God New Years Eve was only a few days away...

Ivy had barely programmed the music for the evening when her doorbell rang.

Jessie and Alina brought a staggering amount of gift boxes and huge bags inside.

"It looks amazing in here," Jessie said, excited. "Thank you so much, Ivy."

"I'm happy to do it. You can't have Christmas in Pinedale without the party."

"True," Jessie agreed. "So, let's get *this* party started."

"I'm all for that."

Together, they placed the gifts under the tree, making sure there would still be space for the ones to come. A few of the guests, like Mark and Kevin, brought children, and they always found a little extra that didn't come from their parents. Everyone, including Ivy, was looking forward to this all year, and when the time arrived, gifts had long been purchased.

"Did you hear from Natasha?" Alina asked. "I read that some flights were canceled."

"Oh no." That would be even worse, to know that she'd be stuck at the airport. "I haven't heard anything yet, so I guess she's on her way."

"It's too bad, but we'll do our best to distract you," Jessie promised.

"She'll be back for New Year's Eve." Ivy meant to mention this casually, but she had no illusions. Her tone and the smile she couldn't keep off her face had to reveal to her friends how she felt about that fact.

"That is so great! I'd say we have a toast, but we still have some work to do."

"Work?" Ivy wondered. "I thought everything is ready?"

"Don't worry, not for you. You sit down and enjoy. Mark and Kevin will be here in a few minutes, and we'll take care of everything."

Ivy didn't understand a thing. Usually, the parties were a potluck mix of whatever people wanted to bring, mostly appetizers, breads and salads and some wine. Given the forced change of plans on this day, it was even more important to keep it uncomplicated.

"I'm confused," she admitted.

"Don't be. We got you covered. You've done so much for us, it's about time we paid you back."

The doorbell rang again, and Jessie went to open to Mark, Kevin, and their daughter Chloe whose eyes widened at the sight of towers of boxes under the tree.

"Some of them are for me?" she asked in a hopeful tone, making the adults laugh.

"For sure, some are," Alina confirmed. "All right people. Let's get cooking."

It turned out that the couple had brought a big bird for the occasion.

Seeing that Ivy was a tad overwhelmed, Kevin reassured her. "Don't worry. We'll clean up later, I promise."

"Wow, this is...Thank you all so much."

Alina and Jessie shared a knowing smile. "No, thank you. You did so much already. Sometimes even Cupid has to take a break to see what's right in front of her. If we can help with that, even better. And we want you to know none of us takes any of it for granted."

"Thank you. I really appreciate it."

The doorbell rang once more. It seemed to Ivy that it was all starting earlier than usual, but apparently her work was already done. She took a look at her phone. Still no news from Natasha.

Chapter Eighteen

NATASHA

Her flight showed as delayed on the board when she hurried inside the terminal—which seemed like a blessing, because she would have never made boarding.

She bought a coffee, bored and antsy at the same time, barely ever taking her eyes off the board as she walked around.

Natasha cringed when the first flights showed as canceled. Hers was still delayed, but her hope was dwindling, given that they all had to leave from the same place.

She took a look around. Only a few travelers were on their way out from Pinedale and other surrounding villages, and she saw the same concern she felt, in their faces. They had probably counted on making it to loved ones last minute...She shook her head to herself, frustrated. She had finished discussing details of the story with Anna via video conference and email before. What was so different now that she needed everyone there in person?

In fact, if there was more of a delay, she might not make it anyway. What was the point?

Natasha studied the designer purses and wallets in one of the stores without really looking at them. When she turned to the board again, her flight and every other one were canceled as well.

Ironic, wasn't it, to think that she didn't want to come to Pinedale in the first place? Natasha had left only reluctantly, but now it looked like she wasn't going anywhere.

Suppressing a swear word, she went to the counter of her airline, where a small line had already formed. They were in the middle of nowhere. Did that mean she had to stay the night?

She could already overhear people in front of her asking for the nearest hotels, and if they would be reimbursed.

Glancing at her watch, Natasha realized that in a matter of minutes, all available cabs might be gone.

"Are we going to get out of here before tomorrow?" a man asked, sounding impatient.

"According to the weather forecast, this could last at least twenty-four hours," the young airline employee told him with a wince, but the man only shrugged.

"Not your fault, I know. Merry Christmas."

"Merry Christmas. I'm sorry, sir. But we can check you in—"

Natasha didn't hear the rest as she headed to the nearest exit, determined to turn this day around. On her way out, she caught a glimpse at a man standing with two women, one of them his age, the other barely past her teens.

I'm starting to hallucinate. It's about time I get home.

The thought brought a warm wonderful feeling, defying the wind driving the snow into her face as she found a cab with a driver ready to take her.

IVY

O ne by one their guests arrived, each of them having tales about traffic coming to a crawl.

"I mean we're used to it, but this is something else," Tina claimed as she put her gifts under the tree and went on to the kitchen. "Wow, it smells amazing. Did you do all of this, Ivy?"

"Just the desserts you saw me bring from the bakery. Mark and Kevin brought the bird, and Alina and Jessie are working on the side dishes. I'm not sure what everyone else is doing."

"More people come every year." Marilyn was beaming. "I think everyone is finding their way here, too. We put a sign on the door."

"How's it going at the museum?" Ivy asked.

"Oh, not too bad. We averted the worst," Marilyn informed her. "Everything is safe and secure now, and the plumber will be back to finish up after Christmas."

"That's a relief."

"It is indeed. Then we can put all the pictures and notes back. Your tree is beautiful, Ivy."

"Thank you. Natasha helped me decorate it."

Marilyn smiled as if this didn't surprise her. "Klara would be so happy to see all this. You'll be sending pictures to your parents?"

"As every year," Ivy confirmed. Truth be told she had almost forgotten about this. The Christmas Eve gathering was important, for Pinedale, everyone in their circle.

Just sometimes she wished that her parents would fly in too and see in person what she had done with the *Magic Christmas Bakery*. She knew that her mother suffered from a fear of flying, and she wouldn't want to put it on them make the drive or take a train ride this long. They appreciated pictures and had told her many times it was fine as long as they could see her during the year.

She suppressed a sigh, taking a look around the many people she loved, and that had found family with one another, some of them rejected by their own families, like Linda and Jocelyn. Some of them finding love in the midst of recovering from chaos, like Lara. Those who came to celebrate what they'd found like an anniversary, and those who had chosen to make Pinedale their home.

Perhaps she could be a little proud, building on her family tradition, to bring them together. She had chosen to do so. Taking in all the happy faces, Ivy knew she'd made the right choice.

Bridget came running over to her.

"Ivy, have you seen this? I'm sure your voicemail and email inbox are overflowing right now."

She cast a glance at the screen, feeling her jaw drop as she tried to understand all the implications.

Hard Work And A Good Heart – The Christmas Cupid Is Real, the headline read. What did that mean? Why did Natasha's boss want her to come to a meeting on Christmas Eve when they had already run the story?

She read more, realizing the lines were starting to blur, and not just because she was tired.

Natasha described how she'd struggled at first to connect a legend with a successful business. *I was ready to find a Scrooge, instead I came to give up my inner Grinch. The owner of the* Magic Christmas Bakery *has a talent far beyond delicious cookies and cakes. She's right at home in Pinedale where a stranger always finds a welcoming place. The romance and the magic of this place are real and have been for generations.*

Ivy skipped to a paragraph closer to the end, distracted by the happy chatter and music around her.

Rumor has it that this year is even more special than others, and the Christmas Cupid should look out for surprise guests at the annual party.

Meanwhile, everyone in town loves this period of the year where they can taste the recipes of Oma Klara, and if they haven't yet, they might find their match over a sweet treat.

The bakery will be open until February 28th, so you have plenty of time to check it out. I recommend you do. Still skeptical? I was, but I'll be home for Christmas.

If you can't get enough of the Christmas Cupid's baked goods, there's more good news: An online shop is in the works. As soon as it's up and running, you'll find all the information you need with us.

Merry Christmas!

Ivy had barely finished the last line when Bridget took the phone from her and handed her a glass of champagne instead.

"You get the gist. Now it's time to celebrate. It's so great that you want to do the online shop. You'll finally be able to quit that other job and do what you love all year long."

"It's very flattering." Ivy felt her face heat before she'd even taken a sip. "But I really don't know about the shop yet. I'd have to do other recipes as well."

133

"Of which you have plenty. I'm sure your grandma baked all year long."

"Oh, yes, she did." Ivy remembered them all, the apple and plum cakes in the fall, the traditional German cheesecake, and one that was for some reason called bee sting cake, the *Bienenstich*. She'd just always assumed that with the way her mother and grandmother had handled the bakery in Pinedale, the *Magic Christmas Bakery*, the task was clear.

What if she could expand her business, to create and sell Oma Klara's recipes all year long? Would she be successful, or would it all take away from the magic?

The one thing Ivy knew was she couldn't make this decision on a whim, and she shouldn't have any more alcohol on a near empty stomach.

"Then all is good," Bridget said. "Come on, let's get you something to eat. I didn't give you enough time to read all of it, but she mentions the knitting circle as well. This is pretty awesome."

Following her to the appetizer buffet, Ivy still wondered who that surprise guest might be. That, and she was thrilled that Natasha had made a promise in front of all her readers.

Next year.

She emptied her glass which was immediately refilled by John passing her by with the bottle.

I'll Be Home for Christmas was playing in the background.

Not everything was a coincidence.

The doorbell rang again.

Chapter Nineteen

NATASHA

She'd sent Anna a text message to explain her situation and then turned her phone off. There was a message from Ivy as well, but she decided she'd answer it in a different way.

Natasha leaned back into the seat of the cab she'd caught, content with herself. It hadn't been hard at all to make that decision. She'd deal with everything else later.

It was Christmas. She made a promise. She'd get to keep it sooner than she thought.

Her thoughts wandered back to the strange moment at the airport, before she left. In a hurry, it didn't occur to her to stop and verify. The man she'd seen looked so much like her father—but for what reason would he be here?

Natasha couldn't hold back the regret when she realized that this year, she hadn't even managed to send a card, too busy with the job, with imagining herself lounging on the beach. She'd never really connected with Martha, her father's second wife, even though he'd met her long after moving out from the family home. Martha had a daughter.

To Natasha, it had all been part of the illusion, and she chose to stay distant.

Recalling her conversation with Ivy, she was wondering what he and Martha were doing this year.

At least Ivy wouldn't have to worry about the same questions. When the knitting circle asked Natasha to help with the Cupid's Christmas present, they had something specific on their minds. Asking her colleague to help with a first draft of the online shop was only a little extra.

"So, Pinedale, huh?" The driver asked, curious. "You might be a little late, but they're big on Christmas. It's really beautiful."

"So I've heard." She was going to give the woman who was helping her get home on this day, in this weather, a huge tip.

IVY

Ivy had always believed that extraordinary things happened in Pinedale, especially around Christmas, but she could hardly believe her eyes when she opened the door to her parents.

She hugged them both and stepped back, perplexed. "How did you get here?"

"By plane, train and then cab," her father laughed. "It's a miracle that last part happened, with the weather here."

"It's not the only miracle. Mom, how did you do that?"

"I'm not sure I know," she admitted. "But we always thought everyone was fine with the way things were until we realized there could be a better way."

"I'm so happy you're here. Please come in and give me your coats, and let's find you a seat. Are you hungry? I'd love to introduce you to everyone."

"That would be lovely, though you know we are familiar with many of them?"

Ivy laughed. "Of course. I'm sorry, it's just a strange day. Strange, but all good."

She was about to get up when Linda and Jocelyn arrived with plates and glasses.

"Marie, David, it's so good to see you again." Linda said. "This Christmas is even more special than the others."

"Especially since we'll all be camping out in Ivy's living room tonight, given how that storm keeps getting worse," Jocelyn commented. "You heard about the article."

"We've read it," Ivy's mother said. "The writer really captured the spirit of the bakery." She shared a smile with her husband. "We hear you are planning to expand? Aside from celebrating Christmas with you, we'd love to talk about that too. We'll help in any way you can."

"Thank you so much."

Ivy couldn't be more blessed, though she took a moment to steal away and check her phone, realizing that all the flights from Natasha's departure airport had been canceled. Had she ever made it out?

She should have insisted. Natasha was the only one missing.

It was quite the surprise—another one—that anyone still managed to make it through the storm, but another car arrived. Two women and one man emerged from it. Since she didn't make all the food, Ivy usually only had a general idea of how many people would be at the party. Guests would invite others. Everyone brought wine, cheese, bread, side dishes and the occasional pie, though Ivy was mainly responsible for dessert. Her prayers that everyone had enough to eat had always been answered, but she was beginning to think they might run out of space.

She went to the window, surprised to see she didn't recognize the family.

Mark joined her by the window. "And here's maybe where our joined meddling with the knitting gals went a little off the rails. We all thought Natasha might change her mind."

"Okay, I love that my parents made it here, but what do these folks have to do with..."

When she turned around, he was already gone. Realization was setting in.

"How did they manage to get them here?" she said out loud, then shook her head with a smile. She didn't need to ask. It was Christmas Eve in Pinedale. With a little luck, they might stay in town until New Year's Eve.

Chapter Twenty

NATASHA

The driver wasn't half as quiet as the one who had driven her to the airport, chatting about a variety of subjects, her family that lived far away, and her previous visits to Pinedale. On any given day, Natasha might have felt irritated and impatient, but once she'd made a decision, calm had settled over her.

She could handle a little conversation.

"This is your first time in Pinedale you said?"

"Technically, it's my second. I was supposed to go back home today. Before, I used to spend the holidays in the Caribbean."

"Oh, really, isn't that strange? No offense, to each their own. But I couldn't imagine Christmas without the snow."

"Even now?" Natasha asked, amused.

"It kind of goes together, don't you think?"

"I must admit all the hot chocolate and cookies I've had were comforting. The beach is too. It's just a different kind of comfort."

"I imagine. We love the holidays, but sometimes it can get a little tiring if there are storms until around March. Then, the Caribbean doesn't seem like such a bad idea."

"It can be a lot of fun, though I don't think I'll do it around Christmas again. What about you? Where would you be if you weren't working tonight?"

"There's no if," the woman said in the same conversational tone. "I don't mind it. It keeps a roof over my head."

"No one waiting for you? Excuse me. That was out of line. I'm incredibly grateful you're driving me in this weather."

"Like I said, it's the job, and no, no one's waiting for me at home. My parents passed away a long time ago. Like I said, there are some cousins far away, but they have their own families. And I haven't found the right person yet...Well, perhaps they aren't out there. It's not a guarantee that there's someone for everyone, right?"

"I used to think that too," Natasha admitted. "Now I'm not so sure...In any case, I don't see how you'll get much more work today, and it is Christmas Eve after all. How would you like spending it with me?"

She had to laugh at the driver's guarded expression.

"I'm sorry, this came out all wrong. You wouldn't believe that I'm a writer. I didn't mean..."

The woman laughed. "Sweetie, no offense, but I didn't think you meant *that*. I'm old enough to be your...well, let's say your mom's older sister."

They both laughed at the odd comparison.

"I'm going to a party to see someone special," Natasha confessed. "There will be lots of friendly people, most of them Pinedale residents, and from what I hear, a ton of food and drinks. Why don't you join us?"

"I don't know..." All joking forgotten, her hesitation couldn't belie the longing in her voice.

"Please say yes. If you know Pinedale, you know they'll treat you like family the moment you set foot in town. It will be fun."

"All right. My name is Donna, by the way. Thank you."

"I'm Natasha, and you're welcome. How long until we get there?"

"Normally? Ten minutes. Now? Thirty would be a success."

"I'm sure there will still be enough of everything."

It occurred to Natasha that they wouldn't be bringing anything, but she hoped Ivy would forgive her.

·♥·♥·♥·♥·♥·

A half hour later, they drove up to the museum. It was hard to see anything through the falling snow, but the building was dark, not even the lights on the wreath outside on. No sign of guests or a party—the lot was empty. With the businesses around closed and no one else on the street, the place looked almost abandoned. What had happened here?

Donna, too, looked perplexed.

"I'm afraid that doesn't look much like a party. Are you sure you have the right address?"

"I am. Wait a minute, I'll go check it out."

Natasha opened the car door and shuddered when the wind drove snow inside the car. Determined, she closed it and went up to the museum's front door, the cold permeating her clothes. She tried the handle, but the entrance was locked. There was no one here. Natasha's heart sank with worry.

Should she go back to the B&B and try to get a room? She had promised Donna a lovely evening. She had such high hopes for herself.

She wasn't willing to give up yet.

"There's really no one here," she said when she got back in the car.

143

"Maybe they decided to cancel because of the weather," Donna reasoned.

"No. They wouldn't do that." Natasha was certain.

Donna didn't argue.

"Where to now?" she asked.

"I can only think of one place."

IVY

"Good evening," she said and reached out to shake the older woman's hand, then that of her husband. "Welcome to Christmas in Pinedale." The two of them, and their daughter, who looked to be in her early twenties, seemed a bit confused at this greeting by a stranger, but they were sticking to the rules.

He held up a bag. "This was a bit on short notice. I hope you don't mind we brought mostly wine and cheeses...and a cherry pie. I know you're a baker, but Natasha loved these as a kid."

"That sounds perfect," Ivy told him as she took the bag from him. "Thank you so much. I'm glad you made it. Your coats can go over there."

The family still appeared cautious.

"Thanks. You probably know that your friends contacted us. I am..."

"Natasha's dad. You must be Martha...and Victoria? They were a bit secretive, but I figured it out." She smiled. "Please, come with me. There's food—lots of food." Finally, they relaxed some, the three of them following her into the living room where Alina waved and pointed out some empty chairs near the buffet. "There's just one thing I need to tell you..." Before she could get to deliver the news that they'd have to wait until New Year's Eve to see Natasha, Marie appeared behind them.

"Martha and Jeff! Is that really you?" she asked, her face lighting up. "This is an amazing surprise. And believe me, I didn't think it would get any more surprising than me getting on a plane. Ivy's friends are magicians in their own right."

"I'd say. When we were told we'd be meeting the Christmas Cupid, no one mentioned it would be our own."

"What?" Ivy asked. She composed herself. "I mean, you two met here?"

He nodded. "I'm not sure what Natasha told you. Her mom and I were long divorced when she died, but it was still a shock. One day, I came here on a business trip. At first, I meant to cancel, but then I thought, why not, I'm going to spend Christmas alone anyway..."

"I had lost a parent the same year," Martha said. "We were both still grieving, but then one day we stood in line at the bakery, and...something happened."

"I can't think of much to say," Ivy admitted, "except...more champagne? And there's still something I need to tell you. Unfortunately..."

Someone had turned up the volume of the Christmas music, so they'd barely heard the doorbell this time. Ivy sought her mother's glance, imploring her to take over. She nodded.

Ivy went to answer the door and nearly fainted but being in Natasha's arms did wonders to keep her upright. She hugged her tightly in return to assure herself she was really here.

"You came back."

"Yes. I realized everything else would be ridiculous, but I must admit I was a bit alarmed to find no one was at the museum..."

"Oh no! The wind must have torn down the sign. Long story," Ivy said when Natasha's confusion showed on her face. "It doesn't matter."

"Ivy..."

"Don't worry, I'll tell you all about it soon. I'm so glad you're here."

"I love you," Natasha blurted out. For a heartbeat or so, she looked startled, jolting Ivy into action. She didn't want her to doubt for a second that Ivy felt the same.

"I love you too. Merry Christmas."

They moved at the same time, leaning in for a sweet, affirming kiss that lasted until they heard someone clear their throat.

"Right. I'm sorry, Donna." Natasha closed the door. "Ivy, I hope you don't mind I brought a guest."

"That's fine. I have a surprise for you too." Holding on to Natasha's hand, Ivy stepped aside, nervous all of a sudden. This year had already brought many unexpected changes and surprises for both of them. Ivy hoped this was a good one for Natasha.

"Natasha," her father said. Martha's smile was both cautious and hopeful, and the younger woman, Martha's daughter, looked intrigued.

"Dad. You're here. How...?"

"It seems like you made a lot of friends in Pinedale in a short time, not that I'm surprised. They wanted to do something nice for you, and I'm so glad they found us. Your article was excellent, and it made us want to come back for those cakes and cookies. Okay, it wasn't just because of that. We wanted to see you."

"Lucky for us," Natasha said, smiling warmly. "Thanks to Donna here, I made it all the way back." She stepped into her father's embrace. Ivy's vision blurred once more when Natasha turned to her and introduced her properly. "I don't know how this is even possible, but I am starting to believe that Ivy really can do magic. Ivy...please meet my dad, Martha, and my...sister Victoria."

From the younger woman's reaction, it was clear that this was the first time Natasha used this term for Martha's daughter, causing happy tears all around.

She'd blame part of it all on the magic of Pinedale and the Christmas Cupid, but the truth was their friends had given both of them more than they could ever pay back.

Chapter Twenty-One

NATASHA

S he would need a bit longer to sort out everything that had happened in Pinedale, especially in the last couple of hours. She hadn't made anything up. The man she'd seen at the airport was her father, and he had come all the way here for a chance to see her this Christmas.

Ivy's mother had, despite her fear of flying, taken a plane with her husband to come celebrate with her daughter. She was the Christmas Cupid who had brought her dad and Martha together.

Natasha had been searching for the usual emotions that were stirred up when she thought of Christmas, her parents' actions, her father finding new love when it seemed impossible for Natasha to move past her grief. Or her irrational resentment for Martha.

She couldn't find any of it. It might be Ivy's hand in hers as they sat at the table, watching a loud and happy crowd celebrating love. Part of it might be the wine, combined with the fire, and the excellent food guests had provided.

Natasha and Donna had caught the end of the appetizer round, and everyone was assembled around the table. Three tables put together, in fact, to make room for everyone. Those who lived in Pinedale had brought chairs as well.

"I swear I didn't know half of it," Ivy whispered to her.

"You have lots of good people in your life."

"You do, too."

Natasha caught Marilyn's smile on her. Whether it was deliberate or a coincidence on Anna's part, Marilyn had been right—her insistence that Natasha do the story had changed everything.

As if on cue, her cell phone vibrated in her pocket. Natasha thought about ignoring it, but changed her mind, only to find Anna's message:

Don't worry about it. Most of the team couldn't make it anyway, and your story is getting out the message quite nicely. We have record traffic! Have a good time. Merry Christmas!

Natasha didn't think Anna would be angry at her, after she had delivered the story her boss had asked for. She felt relieved nonetheless. All the pieces were in place now. She turned her attention back to Ivy.

"So, I kind of knew that they were asking your parents to come. It's quite the energy, two generations of Christmas Cupids, and so many of us who have found love because of them."

"Look who's talking about energy. And thank you for meddling with them behind my back."

"It was my pleasure. I'm sorry I didn't bring anything, but there's one more gift for you somewhere in that pile."

"There is? I would have kept yours until New Year's Eve. I should get it before we get started."

"I'm curious," Natasha admitted.

They both laughed when Mark and Kevin's daughter yawned widely, setting off a chain reaction among the children whose patience was about to run out.

"Yeah, they won't make it much longer. Dessert will be afterwards. I'll be right back."

Natasha used the time to marvel at her surroundings. A house that already felt like a home, where she and Ivy had worked together to get the space ready for the holidays.

Not knowing...

Her eyes welled up when she thought of her mother, the earliest Christmases she remembered, the one she'd tried to forget, and the ones afterwards.

Maybe it was time to acknowledge that both of her parents had done the best they could. Neither had abandoned her on purpose, and they'd always tried to make the holidays as special as possible. She wanted to use the time better. Make an effort to get to know Victoria better. Have the conversations she'd always put off.

And take Ivy to the Caribbean some day because that seemed to be the only way to make her stop working and relax for a bit.

It was also a perfect Valentine's Day destination, and the perfect place to figure out how they would move forward.

But for now, they were in the present, receiving the best gift of all: Being together.

IVY

Having her parents and Natasha at the table was already so much more than she had expected.

Unwrapping the package that held plans to get the *Magic Christmas Bakery* an online store wasn't something she had expected.

"You thought I wrote that without having something to back it up?" Natasha teased.

"Never. But it's all happening at once, and I'm still catching up."

"Don't worry. I'll be here." To demonstrate her point, she kissed Ivy, in front of their parents and all their friends. The future looked beyond promising.

"You mean for the moment. I really appreciate it."

"I mean that my next assignment is romantic vacations in the Caribbean, and while I know a few places, I'd been falling short on the romance part. I had hoped you'd help me out with this once you wrap up the season here."

Ivy could barely believe what she was hearing.

"I'm not sure I'm following."

"I want to be where you are," Natasha said, now serious. "I want you to come with me while I write the story, and we'll figure out what comes next. I hear Pinedale is beautiful all year."

She might still cry tonight, but Ivy had never cried happier tears.

"Merry Christmas," Natasha added, casting a glance at the people around them pretending they weren't listening to their conversation. "I think I finally understand what that means."

·♥·♥·♥·♥·♥·

"Three...Two...One! Happy New Year!"

Ivy and Natasha sealed their wish with a passionate kiss, regardless of their audience. They were ringing in the New Year together as planned, though not exactly as Ivy had imagined. Instead, they were celebrating at Betty's, together with Natasha's dad, his wife and daughter, and Ivy's parents who had shared even bigger news on Christmas.

They planned to move closer to Pinedale to assist Ivy in expanding the bakery to an all-year venture.

Before the New Year started, Ivy's mother had cleared up a long-held superstition.

"Mom loved Pinedale during the holidays, but there was more she wanted to discover. It didn't mean anything else. Sure, the legend refers to Christmas, but I'm sure Klara's recipes will attract people all year long. You remember her apple cake and the *Bienenstich*?"

"Of course. I never figured out what it had to do with bees, but it was delicious."

"Another legend. Apparently, the honey on the cake attracted bees, and the baker who invented it was stung. Imagine if people had stopped making it...I think it's time to expand.

Holding on to a good thing is always a good idea, and it should go beyond the magic of Christmas."

Ivy couldn't help smiling at Natasha, something that didn't go unnoticed with her mother.

"Business and love. Let's have a toast to an amazing New Year."

Around the table, everyone raised their glasses.

This New Year's Eve wasn't at all what Ivy had expected when she'd come up to Pinedale this year. It was so much better.

Epilogue

IVY

B efore heading to the airport, they had one more stop to make: She and Natasha walked into the museum, where Marilyn had resumed business. Many of the guests who had stayed after Christmas, had helped restoring the wall of joy. Ivy and Natasha had done their share.

"You two must be so excited," Marilyn said. "Thank you for coming by."

"We brought you something."

In the past few days, Ivy had experimented with different recipes from Oma Klara's notes, one of them the traditional German cheesecake.

"This is so lovely."

"There will be more after we come back," Ivy promised. "Mom will finish up the season for me. When we re-open, it will be full-time. Can you imagine? The family who runs the Italian restaurant will move, and they were wondering how to break it to me…The timing is perfect. You will also be able to order online—"

"But first it will be time for a bit of rest," Natasha reminded her gently. "Thanks for everything, Marilyn. There's just one more thing."

"Of course."

Marilyn followed them up the stairs where she pointed out an empty spot on the wall, not an easy venture. "Is this okay?"

"Perfect," Natasha said, and pinned the selfie they'd printed out, on the wall.

The sight made Ivy smile so hard it almost hurt: The two of them at the Christmas party, radiating pure happiness.

It could come true for everyone—even the Christmas Cupid herself.

NATASHA

This had usually been one of the busiest times of the year. Natasha wasn't entirely idle as she was typing away on her laptop on the balcony of their rental, her skin caressed by the ocean breeze. When she looked up, she saw the ocean, palm trees swaying.

She had never been dismissive of the holiday as she'd been of Christmas. She simply didn't have much time or use for it, and her stories around that time were typically more anti-Valentine's Day, reminding readers what else was happening in the world.

You Can't Buy Happiness, But A Little Getaway To Paradise Is Worth It.

"How's it going?" Ivy asked. Natasha turned around to see her standing in the doorway, holding a couple of colourful, fruity cocktails.

"Well enough to call it a day. How about we take those in the hammock?"

Ivy's smile was all the confirmation she needed.

She didn't have to dream anymore. All of her dreams had come true.

About the Author

B arbara Winkes writes sapphic crime drama and Christmas romance. She loves writing characters who get the job done, whether it's stopping a predator or saving cherished traditions—while still making time for love. She lives with her wife in Quebec City.

barbarawinkes.com

Also by Barbara Winkes

Bells Will Be Ringing
A Girlfriend for Christmas
Destination Christmas, Next Stop Love
The Christmas Memory